MAKING
A
PLAY

Also by Abbi Glines

The Field Party Series
Until Friday Night
Under the Lights
After the Game
Losing the Field

MAKING A PLAY

A Field Party Novel

BY

ABBI GLINES

Simon Pulse

NEW YORK   LONDON   TORONTO   SYDNEY   NEW DELHI

SIMON PULSE

An imprint of Simon & Schuster Children's Publishing Division
1230 Avenue of the Americas, New York, New York 10020
First Simon Pulse hardcover edition August 2019
Text copyright © 2019 by Abbi Glines
Jacket photo-illustration copyright © 2019 by We Monsters
Jacket photograph of sky copyright © 2019
by Getty Images/Robert Galeno
Jacket photograph of bleachers and field copyright © 2019
by Gallery Stock/Dale May
All rights reserved, including the right of reproduction
in whole or in part in any form.
SIMON PULSE and colophon are registered trademarks
of Simon & Schuster, Inc.
For information about special discounts for bulk purchases,
please contact Simon & Schuster Special Sales at 1-866-506-1949
or business@simonandschuster.com.
The Simon & Schuster Speakers Bureau can bring authors to your live
event. For more information or to book an event contact the
Simon & Schuster Speakers Bureau at 1-866-248-3049
or visit our website at www.simonspeakers.com.
Series designed by Jessica Handelman
Jacket designed by Heather Palisi
Interior designed by Mike Rosamilia
The text of this book was set in Stempel Garamond LT.
Manufactured in the United States of America
2 4 6 8 10 9 7 5 3 1
Library of Congress Cataloging-in-Publication Data
Names: Glines, Abbi, author.
Title: Making a play / by Abbi Glines.
Description: First Simon Pulse hardcover edition. |
New York : Simon Pulse, 2019. | Series: A Field party novel |
Summary: In the small town of Lawton, Alabama, high school senior
Ryker, a player on and off the football field, falls in love with a deaf girl
who lives with an overprotective twin brother and a bigoted father.
Identifiers: LCCN 2019006317 | ISBN 9781534403925 (hardcover)
Subjects: | CYAC: Dating (Social customs)—Fiction. | Love—Fiction. |
High schools—Fiction. | Schools—Fiction. | African Americans—
Fiction. | Deaf—Fiction. | People with disabilities—Fiction.
Classification: LCC PZ7.G4888 Mak 2019 | DDC [Fic]—dc23
LC record available at https://lccn.loc.gov/2019006317
ISBN 9781534403949 (eBook)

To my niece, Olivia Potts, who reads these books before they ever hit the shelves. I can't ever tell you how proud I am of you. As your second year of college begins, soak in every moment and make memories that will last forever.

This Field Is Mine—
Might Want to Remember That

CHAPTER 1

RYKER

The view from the back of the pickup truck was pretty damn sweet. Like every Friday night, the bonfire was blazing, music was pumping, and the people I'd grown up with in this town were all here. Most importantly, my cousin, Nash, was here. Smiling, with his arm around Tallulah, who I credited for helping him find himself after his injury. He'd coached tonight at the game. He couldn't play, but he had been there on the sidelines, yelling at us, cursing like a fucking sailor. Made me grin, thinking about it. The win had made it perfect.

Losing a defense coordinator after only a few games could have been bad, but Dace hadn't been liked by anyone.

His ass belonged in jail. Nash taking over his place on the field had been the best thing Coach Rich could have done for us. It made the team complete with Nash out there again.

"Ryker," a female voice called from below. I turned my gaze to the ground and saw Nova Cox grinning up at me. She'd been flirting for a few weeks now, and I'd been letting her work for it. She was smoking hot. A transfer last year from someplace in Tennessee. I couldn't remember where. She'd told me, but I hadn't paid much attention. This year, so far, had been pretty wrapped up with getting Nash out of the damn, dark hole he'd crawled in after he was told he'd never play football again.

Shifting my gaze once more just to be sure he was good, I caught him kissing Tallulah with her arms around his neck. He was fine. More than fine. He'd battle his demons for a while still. I'd never seen someone die, but he'd seen death up close. I'd still need to keep an eye on him, but for now he looked pretty damn happy. I could ease off some of my protecting him and let Tallulah change his world.

It was time I enjoyed my senior year. So far it'd been shit. Nothing like I had imagined. I loved playing football, and I knew it was going to be what paid for my college. But it wasn't my life. Not like it had been for Nash.

I wanted something more. I just wasn't sure what that

was yet. But I wanted a life that meant something. Made me feel like I had made a difference.

"Come down from your throne and party with the rest of us," Nova cooed up at me, batting her long eyelashes that I would bet about fifty bucks weren't real. Her creamy-mocha skin looked really damn attractive in the moonlight. With a shrug, I walked to the tailgate and jumped down right in front of her. She giggled, and it wasn't annoying. That was a plus.

"That beer?" I asked, reaching for her red plastic cup.

She scrunched her nose up. "Ewww, no. It's a margarita. Blakely brought two gallons of some mixed up."

I let go of the cup. That shit sounded nasty. "I need a beer," I told her, and turned back to the keg on the truck bed to get me some.

"Rumor is you don't want Blakely here, but Nash made you let her come for Hunter's sake," Nova said.

Girls and their gossip. I didn't like Blakely. She'd hurt Nash when he was down. But it was the second best thing that happened to him, getting rid of her, Tallulah being the best. I shrugged and took a drink. "Don't care if she's here or not."

That was the truth. As long as I wasn't subjected to talking to her, I was good. I'd never thought much of her when Nash was with her either.

Nova moved in closer to me and made sure to press her breast against my arm. She liked her chest size and made sure to push those things up so everyone else could see them and admire them too. I wasn't complaining. She was welcome to press them on me if she wanted.

"You seem more relaxed tonight. Not so uptight and tense. I like this side of you. I haven't seen it since last spring."

I lifted my left shoulder slightly, one for an acknowledgment of her words, and the other to get a rub on those boobs she was pressing on me. They seemed real. She wasn't stuffing the things when she jacked them up. I hadn't been sure how much of her was fake. She had the lashes, and I knew that hair was too damn perfect to be all hers. It looked good on her, though.

"I've been preoccupied with Nash. But it seems his luck has turned."

Her hand slid across my chest as she turned toward me. "He seems happy." Her voice had dropped to a sexy purr, and it was nice. She rolled her assets over my chest as she moved to stand in front of me. I spread my legs slightly in my stance so she would easily fit up against my body. Attraction with her was not an issue, and I knew she could feel it against her stomach. No way she could miss it. A small grin spread over her full lips, and I decided it was time to taste them. See if this was going to be as fun as it was promising.

Leaning down, I took a slight nibble on her lower lip and pulled its juicy plumpness into my mouth to suck it before going in for a full taste test. The sweet margarita was mixed with the mint from her gum, and it worked. It was girly and sexy.

I rested my hands on her hips and pulled her closer to me. She wiggled against my arousal and thoughts of taking this back into the woods and away from the whole damn field party's viewing pleasure sounded like a wise idea.

"Ohmygod, just get a damn backseat somewhere. No one wants to see that." Blakely's familiar, annoying voice was like ice over my head, but I only broke the kiss. I kept Nova up against me.

"This field is mine. Might want to remember that." The threat in my tone was cold. I wanted it to be.

Blakely tossed her long blond hair over her shoulder and rolled her eyes. "I'm with Hunter." She said it as if it made her safe. Dating the quarterback was the only reason she was here. At least she knew it. But Hunter was a junior. He wasn't originally from here, and we played well together on the field, but he was not one of my boys. This wouldn't save her ass if she pissed me off.

"Don't give a fuck," I replied. "If he wants to leave

with you, he can, but he won't stop me from sending your ass off."

She opened her mouth to say something more, but Nova interrupted her. "Looks like he's already gone. Running." Nova sounded pleased. "Guess he was waiting until you walked off to make his escape."

I turned to see Hunter in a full-out sprint, headed toward the clearing where everyone parked. Nova wasn't exaggerating. The dude was moving. I doubted he was running from Blakely. I was more than positive he'd been looking forward to getting laid tonight. Blakely was well known for being easy.

"What the fuck?" Blakely's tone, however, did make me smile. Whatever his reasons for running, she wasn't happy about it.

"Damn, bitch, what did you do to him?" Nova drawled, enjoying this a little too much. Girls could be vicious. In a fight, though, I knew Nova would take Blakely out fast. She may not be from around here, but I could tell by the way she carried herself that she was not a female you wanted to tie up with. She'd lived a much different life from me. Her parents weren't around much. From what she said, I knew her grandmother had raised her. Once she'd mentioned her dad being in jail. I didn't ask her any questions, because I wasn't sure I wanted to hear the answers. My home life was a fairy tale compared to hers.

Blakely glared at Nova, and I watched as Nova straightened, then turned from me to Blakely. Nova cocked her head to the side, and the threatening gleam in her eyes made me a little nervous. "You want some?" she asked with no emotion. Then she crooked her finger at Blakely in a *come and get it* way.

Holy fuck.

The fear in Blakely's eyes quickly replaced the anger. She backed up a step and shook her head. "No. Jesus, what's your issue?" Her tone was a bit shaky as she tried to keep her cool. I felt a little sorry for her, and that was surprising even to me. Blakely spun and stalked off, walking faster with each step down the same path Hunter had just taken.

From the looks of how fast he'd been moving, I didn't think he'd be there when she arrived, unless he had been getting something from his car.

Nova's shoulders relaxed, and she turned back to me with a seductive grin as if nothing had happened. Her eyes were like caramel, and before this moment, I'd thought they held a kindness and warmth. Now I saw the fight there. I wondered where that came from.

"I'm not against finding a backseat. Your truck doesn't

have a big enough one, though," she said, then took her fingertip and ran it down my chest until she reminded me exactly what I had been feeling before our interruption.

This was going to be easier than I'd expected. Nova had been tossing it around willingly, from what I'd heard, but it had all been college guys. I was the first guy her age that she seemed interested in. I figured college guys had probably taught her a lot.

"Where'd Hunter run off to?" Nash called out in my direction as if I had been the one to send him running.

I shrugged. "Been preoccupied. Don't give a fuck where the QB went. But my guess is getting the hell away from his date."

Nash rolled his eyes at me, but I could see he was trying not to laugh. I smirked at his attempt, and that got a grin out of him.

"If the two of you are done with your humor, we can go find a spot . . . alone now," Nova said, placing a hand on my left cheek and turning my face back in her direction. She was brave. No self-confidence issues with this one. That was for damn sure.

"Okay, yeah, I got a place," I told her, and shot one more glance at Nash. He was watching us with amusement, and I saluted him before taking Nova and walking away.

Nova was fun. There were times I saw the way Nash

looked at Tallulah or she looked at him, and I wanted that. Or I thought I did for a moment. Then I remembered that I was living the life right now. I didn't have time for that kind of shit. I didn't need to use my truck. There was an empty barn waiting on us.

I Didn't Fit in That World,
But I Was Happy in Mine

CHAPTER 2

AURORA

Make this fast. If you are listening, God, just please let it all go so quickly it can't be painful. You didn't hear the last couple prayers I shot your way, but maybe you could make up for it now. Today would be perfect.

The hand on my shoulder didn't startle me. I knew it was Hunter. My twin brother. If anyone was dreading this more than me, it was him. I could see the worry in his eyes. I didn't have to hear his voice. But then I'd never heard his voice. I read his emotions well. The anxiety pulsing through him was even in the gentle squeeze on my shoulder. It had been elementary school since we'd gone to school together.

He was angry at our mother. Not because he didn't want me here, but because he feared what this would be like for me. His face had been red as he'd yelled words I couldn't read quickly enough, but I did catch a couple of curse words when my mother showed up with me and my things at our father's house Friday night. He had gotten in Mom's face, and Dad had pulled him back. It had been so ugly.

That night he'd sat with me in my new room in our comfortable silence. Both of us reading a book, not needing to do anything more than be near each other. I knew he was scared for me. My earliest memories were of Hunter protecting me. He sat with me because it was all he knew to do. He thought Mom had caused me emotional pain, and he was trying to make it better. Just by being there.

The doors to Lawton High School stopped us, and I turned my head to look at Hunter. His jaw was fixed in a clenched position. His eyes serious and determined. He reminded me of someone about to go to war. I reached out and patted his hand.

"I am going to be fine," I said, hoping I hadn't talked loud. I didn't use my voice around anyone outside my family. When you can't hear yourself, it's intimidating. Although Hunter swore I sounded fine and my words were clear, I also knew he'd lie to me to protect me.

He inhaled deeply and let his gaze take in the surround-
ings, as if he was ready to pounce on any sign of danger. The
idea of me going to a regular high school was scary for both of
us. But if I was going to keep Hunter from being a complete
wreck, I had to act confident. I didn't feel it, but I could act it.

"I'm a text away." He said the words, knowing I could
read his lips easily. I'd been doing it for most of our lives. Some
people's lips were hard to read, but not his. I knew him as well
as I knew myself. When we were in a heated discussion and
talking too fast for me to read his lips, he'd sign. But most of
the time we talked with our voices when communicating.

I nodded, not wanting to use my voice anymore with
the other students rushing past us. I saw a guy stop and slap
Hunter on the back. I couldn't see his mouth clearly from
the angle he was at, so I wasn't sure what he was saying.
Hunter was forcing a smile and saying something. I could
see his head move with the motions. The guy was taller than
Hunter and had the most amazing blue eyes I'd ever seen.
His brown skin was beautiful, and the big smile he flashed
my way showed a set of perfect white teeth. He was a nice
guy. His eyes said so. I was good at reading faces, expressions, especially eyes. They were the window to your soul,
if only someone looked closely.

"I didn't know Hunter had a sister. Nice ---- you.
I'm ----" I got most of his words. I could piece together

what he meant. I didn't get his name, though. It wasn't something I was familiar with. Naz, maybe? That would be extremely unique if it was. But somehow I doubted it.

This was the moment I could use my voice or nod and smile, then let Hunter explain why I wasn't talking back. I wanted to be brave enough to talk, but I couldn't bring myself to do it. Besides, I wasn't positive what he said his name was.

Hunter was talking again, his head turned toward the guy, Naz or whatever. I saw the guy's eyes widen as Hunter explained I couldn't hear. He seemed unsure, and I knew he would inevitably feel awkward. Hunter was good at dealing with that, too. Again I wasted my thoughts on wishing my mother hadn't met Lou and decided to move to California with him. I'd missed my dad and Hunter, but I also missed the security of the life I'd had with Mom in North Carolina.

A stunning blonde walked up beside the guy, and he put his arm around her waist. Her gaze moved to me, and I prepared to get the pitied, annoyed, impatient glare I knew from past experiences with beautiful girls like her. Instead the pure, genuine kindness in her eyes took my breath away a little. I was normally good at reading people quickly. I'd seen her outward beauty and assumed the worst. She glanced at Hunter a moment as he said something to her, then her eyes softened before she walked around the guy she was with, to get closer to me.

"Hello, Aurora. I'm Tallulah. I'm so happy to meet you. Do you have a phone? We could exchange numbers. You can text me if you need any help today finding things. Or want to hide in the library with me. It's my special place." She signed all of that. Perfectly.

She'd shocked me twice now. I liked her. The first relief I'd felt since waking up this morning knowing what I was about to face. I reached for my phone in my jeans pocket and handed it to her. She did the same. We quickly added our numbers in each other's phones. When I handed hers back, I then signed, "Thank you. I could use a friend. How do you know how to sign?" I had to ask. It was rare, unless one had a family member who was deaf.

She beamed at me. "I spent a lot of time reading. Alone. For most of my life. I'm not very social. I taught myself how to sign three summers ago with two different books I checked out of the library. I also watched YouTube lessons. Then I volunteered at an after-school daycare for the hearing impaired in an underprivileged area. I found out about it on a Google search. I went to read to them three times a week that summer. Until they had to close due to lack of funding." When she signed the last, she seemed heartbroken. Her eyes were so sad. She was a walking contradiction. How was someone who looked like a Barbie doll not social?

Hunter's hand touched my arm, and I looked up at

him. "We need to get to the office to get you all checked in. You can text Tallulah and meet up with her later. Y'all can be recluses in the library together." He said the last bit with a grin. A relieved, very grateful grin. He was surprised by Tallulah too. I had the feeling he didn't know her well, although he seemed to know her boyfriend.

I turned back to Tallulah. "I'll text you if I get lost," I signed.

She held up her phone, then said, "You better," with her mouth, realizing I could read her lips.

I felt Hunter's entire frame relax. He'd been strung so tight all morning. I grinned up at him, understanding. He winked, and we headed into the office. Dad had said everything was transferred this morning. He'd come by on his way to work to fill out the paperwork and check things out. He had drilled Hunter with so many things last night, I had finally stepped in and begged him to stop. Hunter was already worried enough. He didn't need any extra stress.

I could do this. They all needed to calm down. I hadn't wanted to be put in the hearing-impaired school when they moved me to it in second grade. I wanted to be with Hunter. I had cried for the first two weeks because I missed him. We had rarely been apart, and he had been my security blanket. But then life was easier. I learned more. I caught up with where I should have been academically. I'd fallen behind at the regular school, and this new school became my second home. My family.

When our parents divorced and Dad moved here, taking Hunter with him, four years ago, I'd once again fallen apart. But I had agreed with them that I needed my school. I was too scared to do anything else. I didn't know Hunter's world anymore. I knew he had a lot of friends. He was good at football. Girls liked him.

I didn't fit in that world, but I was happy in mine. My thoughts now went to Denver. We hadn't broken up, but I knew the distance was going to make it inevitable. He was my first and only boyfriend. We had been together since seventh grade. He had been there for me when Hunter moved away. Then we'd slowly become something more than friends. Leaving him had been hard too.

Hunter stopped at the front desk in the office, and the lady behind it looked from him to me and smiled before looking back at Hunter.

"Yes. I have her schedule here. Her locker is three-thirty-three. I made sure it was close to yours. If you need anything or Aurora needs anything, do not hesitate to come see me. We are here to help." I read her lips easily, and I got the feeling she was talking loudly by the wide expressions she was making with her eyes. Hunter's back had straightened some when she started speaking too, as if he was surprised. That normally meant someone was yelling for my benefit. Not that it helped me at all. It was human nature.

Hunter said something, then turned to me and rolled his eyes as he held up the paper in his hand. I had guessed correctly She'd been talking very loud. I glanced around the office to see the other three students in there staring in our direction. However, they weren't studying me. All three were female, and all three were looking at Hunter with obvious longing. I bit back a smile and shot an amused glance his way. He was reading my schedule, completely oblivious to the hearts he was breaking in his uninterested response.

We had just stepped out of the office when a very angry female stopped in front of us. Her eyes were blazing, her hands on her hips. Skin showing where her shirt didn't quite meet the top of her very short skirt. Could girls come to school dressed like this? Her glare was directed at me as her red lips lifted in a snarl. There was an evil in her eyes. A cold bitterness was there too. She wasn't a nice person, but she had some pain hidden underneath.

"Who the FUCK is she?" the girl demanded. Her words easy to read.

If this was the girl Hunter was dating, then he had his hands full. She was one hot minute away from crazy.

CHAPTER 3

RYKER

Another fucking Monday. Everyone rushing inside before the last bell, white girls with their Starbucks coffee cups in hand taking selfies with each other outside, and Blakely yelling at someone just inside the entrance.

I didn't even give that a second look, because my guess was that Hunter was getting his balls handed to him for his escape Friday night. Blakely had come back, gotten drunk, and passed out, and Asa had hauled her ass home, carrying her over his shoulder. She puked on his feet. I missed it all, but that was the recap I'd got from Nash. Asa was a nice guy, but he loved his Chevy truck. He'd had to pay for half of it. His dad was tough. So after she puked on his feet and her clothing, she was put in the bed of his truck for the ride home. That shit made me laugh.

Nova had been more than happy to take things to the old barn at the back of our property. But I didn't let it go as far as she was willing. Something didn't seem right. She was too desperate. Too willing to get naked with a guy she barely knew. It had been hard, but after some playing around, I'd told her to get dressed and then offered to take her home. She'd been a little pissed and told me she had her own car and didn't need a man to drive her.

I sat there on the old tractor tire long after she'd walked out. She had a body, and I was attracted to her, but I was attracted to most girls with hot bodies. Sleeping with them because it was easy didn't seem to bother me before. With Nova, something was odd. I didn't feel comfortable with her level of neediness. Or willingness. I doubted I'd grown morals suddenly, but I had stopped things.

My eyes scanned the area for Nova. I wanted to see her again and make sure it hadn't been the beer that messed with my head. There was still time to save the situation. My momma swore she was gonna raise a gentleman, but I had a few more parties and panties to get into before that happened. Not today, Momma. Not. Today.

The late bell sounded, and those not yet moving toward

the hallways broke into runs while Principal Haswell's voice called out loudly, "No running!"

Everyone's pace turned into a fast walk, and I sighed, not worrying about being late for class. I'd rather find Nova and see if my moment of chivalry, or whatever the hell it had been, was the end to a chance with her.

"Blakely, get to class. Now." Haswell's voice carried, and I had to turn to see what had happened with that clusterfuck. Hunter was going to figure out she was poison sooner or later. From his sprinting off Friday night, I was assuming it was sooner.

The amused grin that had started to spread on my face froze, and I stopped walking. My eyes were locked on someone else's. I'd never seen green like that before. I wasn't sure there was an adequate description for that color green. But Jesus they were piercing. Like they could read your soul. Then she blinked, and it broke the spell. Startled by my odd reaction, I took in the rest of the person that came with those eyes. Pink lips that looked almost heart shaped from here, a small nose, high cheekbones, creamy pale skin with freckles—and for some reason that made me smile. I liked the freckles. A long strand of hair . . . it wasn't just red but more copper in color . . . curled against her bare arms.

She was like a perfect pixie standing there . . . beside Hunter fucking Maclay? I tore my eyes off her and took in the rest of the scene. Blakely was calmed down now, and Hunter was talking to her with a disgusted scowl on his face. I wasn't concerned with them, but the redhead had my interest. I looked back at her and saw she was no longer looking at me but watching Hunter speak, as if every word out of his mouth was golden.

If that was why he'd bailed on Blakely, I was either going to high-five him or toss him in a closet to get him away from her. She was new, and it wasn't fair he had laid a claim on her before anyone else had even got a look at her. I was more than positive that if I got her alone in a barn, I wouldn't be sending her home.

Hunter took her arm and walked around Blakely. "I need to get her to class. We'll talk later," he said loud enough that I heard him. He was leading the new girl around Blakely, who now seemed to be panicking a bit and flashing a fake smile at the girl. What the fuck was going on with all that?

The girl was studying Blakely as if she felt sorry for her. Genuinely sorry. Not a pity glance. My stomach tightened. My chest felt weird. But something about that girl was affecting me. I didn't care that Hunter's hand was on her in a rather protective way. He needed to be ready for some competition. She was having to hurry to keep up with Hunter, and I didn't like the way he was pulling her along like a child. That annoyed me.

I began moving in their direction, without thinking about what I was going to do or say, when she turned those eyes toward me again. Jesus Christ, it was like a boulder slammed into me. I was frozen again. Staring at her. Just when I was about to question my sanity, she smiled. Straight white teeth. As perfect as the rest of her. The purity of that smile was in her eyes. Nothing was there clouding it. Making you wonder what she was thinking or up to. It was the most real thing I'd ever experienced in my life.

Hunter's gaze swung to me. He still looked annoyed and very focused. But he nodded his head. "Hey, Ryker" was all he said, not stopping. Her gaze was back on him now. She was staring up at him. She only came to his shoulders.

"You have Literature first. But it's okay that you're late. I will explain. It's a substitute anyway. They fired the Lit teacher a couple weeks ago," he said to her.

She frowned, looking confused, and then fell into a quicker pace beside him. Just before they turned the corner, she glanced back over her shoulder at me and gave me one more smile.

Holy fuck. How did she do that? It was like a bolt of lightning in my chest, and I wanted more of it.

A locker door slammed, snapping me out of my sudden haze. Blakely stalked passed me without a word, thank God.

The hallway was empty now, and I was going to be late to class. I wasn't in the mood for people yet anyway. I turned and headed back to the office. Mrs. Murphy would give me a late pass, fuss at me a moment; it would kill some time.

When I reached the office door, the ancient metal box fan was blowing, Mrs. Murphy was making announcements, and it smelled like coffee and fall candles. Halloween decorations had been replaced with Give Thanks and Harvest instead. It was like someone had robbed the Dollar Store holiday section.

I waited as she finished her spiel with a "GO LIONS!" then turned to me and sighed. "Ryker, why can't you get yourself to class on Mondays?"

I smirked at her. "Because it just wouldn't start my week right without seeing your beautiful smile, Mrs. Murphy."

She beamed at me, and her weathered cheeks blushed. She'd been here when my parents had gone to high school. I wondered if she loved it here as much as she acted like it. I figure at her age you can't fake that kind of joy.

"Charismatic, like your daddy, for sure," she said, shaking her head and writing out a late slip for me. "Get on to class. You're missing good learning time."

I wasn't missing anything. It took a good twenty minutes before any first-period teacher even woke up enough to get going. They'd let us sit there on our phones while they drank coffee and pretended to be working on something. When we all knew they were on Facebook.

I stopped just before I left the office and turned back to Mrs. Murphy. "Who is the new girl?" I asked her. I needed a name. Something.

She smiled so softly and gently, as if the reminder of the girl made her happy. Interesting. Maybe she was a witch with powers to entrance. "Aurora Maclay. Hunter's *twin* sister. Sweet, sweet girl."

My cheeks should have cracked from the grin that spread over my face. It was his sister. Halle-*fuckin'*-lujah.

He's Not Always . . . Nice

CHAPTER 4

AURORA

"Ryker Lee. He's on the team, wide receiver, best one we have, but don't even think about it," Hunter said firmly as we reached the door to the class I was about to enter. He said I had his schedule, which I think relieved and concerned him.

"I didn't ask you," I said, using my voice since we were alone in the hallway now.

"I saw you looking back at him. He's with a new girl all the time. You are not his type. He likes easy girls. Besides, you're still with Denver, right?"

I nodded. For now.

"He was looking at me," I said in my defense.

"All guys look at you. That's part of my stress," he said, then reached for the door.

"They won't once they know." I said the words before thinking about it.

Hunter tensed. He hated it when I said things like that. "If it matters, they aren't worthy." He didn't say any more. I knew the rest. He'd said it all a million times.

He walked into the room, then held the door open for me to follow. I went in and didn't make eye contact with anyone else. I tended to stare too long. Eyes intrigued me. Understanding people always drew me in.

I watched as Hunter spoke to the substitute teacher. I wondered why the Literature teacher had been fired. The substitute smiled at me and said something to the class. Hunter nodded his head for me to follow him. He took us to the far right of the room, and I sat down in front of him when he pointed at it.

I pulled out my laptop and placed it on the desk like the other students in the room. Hunter tapped my shoulder, then held up his phone. I took mine from my pocket, and his text popped up with a website for me to log in to. A piece of paper slipped over my shoulder, and on it was the login info for me with my student ID and a password.

I followed the instructions, not looking up to see what the rest of the class was doing. My phone vibrated, and I looked down at it to see another text from Hunter.

She's talking. I told her you could read lips if she kept her face visible to you and didn't talk too fast.

I jerked my gaze up to see the teacher in the front, looking directly at me as she spoke. I caught most words and wrote notes if I needed to remember to ask Hunter about something later when I was unsure. The class was currently covering *Society and Solitude* by Ralph Waldo Emerson. I'd already read this and studied it at my former school. I let out a little sigh of relief. I wasn't going to be behind in here.

She asked questions, and none of them were challenging. At least not in my opinion. But then she was a substitute. I doubted she had read the book. Others were raising their hands and answering, although I wasn't going to stare at them to see what their answers were. I would just watch the teacher's response. This was my favorite subject, and I loved Emerson. Not being able to say anything and discuss it in class was going to be tough, but if this was the hardest thing I faced, it would be fine. Until they got a new Literature teacher, the class discussions wouldn't be helpful anyway.

Is this going to work? Can you follow along okay?

The text from Hunter caught my attention. But the teacher was talking about the perspective, and I didn't want to miss this. She had an iPad in front of her she was reading off, and she kept forgetting to look up for my sake. I had to focus hard on her mouth or what I could see of it. I didn't respond to Hunter's text, I just nodded my head for him and kept studying the teacher's mouth the best that I could. When she got too distracted, I couldn't follow along, because she talked fast. But she'd see me and remember and slow down. They were letting me try it this way for now. It was going to take that long to get the computer program the county supplied into their system for hearing-impaired students. That was the information Dad had texted me this morning after he had come here and talked to the office.

I was the first one this school had since the new laptop system had been put in place. Dad had looked for a hearing-impaired school within driving distance, but so far he'd had no luck. The closest was two hours away. He had spent most of his weekend on the internet and the phone, trying to figure out how to handle my being here.

Dad had said in his text that they had told him the computer program hadn't been successful with all students who had used it. I was going to prove to them all I could and would do this. I had a little over a year and a half left. It would take extra work, but I could manage. Besides, the real world wasn't going to be as accommodating.

The next seventy minutes went quickly as I struggled to

make out what the substitute was saying. When everyone stood up, I closed my laptop and stood up too. Hunter was tucking his laptop in his backpack, watching me closely. "You good?" he asked.

I nodded and smiled.

He seemed tense still. Like he didn't believe me. "Let's go," he said, then took my laptop and stuck it in my bag, and we headed for the door.

The moment he stepped out the door, the girl Hunter was dating was there. I stepped back, a little frightened of her. She was in his face again, and he was trying to get around her. I backed up to give him room and noticed others were watching and listening. Hunter hated this kind of thing. I was going to find out how he had gotten hooked up with her this evening. Had he not smelled the crazy on her?

Hunter's angry expression swung to someone behind me. "She's my sister, Rifle. Back off." I spun around to see a very broad-shouldered guy with curly dark blond hair and brown eyes looking at Hunter then back at me. I hadn't realized anyone was behind me.

He seemed friendly. "Didn't know you had a sister," the guy said.

Hunter responded, because the guy's gaze shifted to him. He held up both hands and said, "Chill, man."

This wasn't helping me fit in. I gave Rifle—whose name

I would have questioned, but I could read my brother's lips too well; I knew without a doubt he'd called the guy Rifle—a small apologetic smile, then turned to Hunter and scowled at him. If we were alone, I'd let him have it.

He returned my scowl and said something to Blakely, who was still there; then he took my arm and pulled me through the crowd. I was getting a little tired of the leading-me-around thing. I wasn't a child. He knew I didn't like being treated differently, yet he was doing it. I was trying to understand that he was having a hard time with this too. But I was going to have to lay some ground rules. I waited until we rounded the corner before jerking my arm from his grip. He stopped and turned to me.

"What?" he asked, confused.

I held up my arm he'd been hauling me around by and shot him a pointed look.

His shoulders dropped, and he pinched his temple the way he did when he was frustrated. When his hand fell away, he said, "I'm sorry."

I nodded. He should be. I wanted to tell him to go. Let me do this alone. I wasn't here to be a burden on him. I hated the idea of that.

Tallulah appeared to his left and smiled at me.

"Can I have her schedule?" she asked Hunter, keeping her face turned toward me so I could read her lips.

He frowned. "Why?"

"Because you two look stressed. I think she needs a little space, and you need to relax."

I couldn't agree more, and I was so thankful for this angelic-looking person.

"We have almost every class together. I can take her," he argued.

I started to say something, without thinking about using my voice, when Tallulah spoke up. "She doesn't need her brother taking her around all day. Give me the schedule. And let us get to know each other."

Naz then appeared beside her and kissed her cheek. His head was turned, and I couldn't see his lips, but whatever he said, Hunter handed over the schedule with a sigh in response. Tallulah took it, shot Hunter a beaming grin, then kissed Naz quickly on the lips.

"Let's go," she said to me. Although I couldn't hear her, I knew her voice must be chipper and happy. It sure made Naz smile.

She walked beside me down the hallway. I found myself searching for the guy from earlier. I wanted to ask her about Ryker. Maybe I would get a chance later.

Her hand touched my wrist, and she pointed to my right. I looked in the direction she was pointing to see Rifle there, smiling at me again. I turned back to her, and she raised her eyebrows. "Rifle seems happy to see you. Have you met him?" she asked.

I nodded. We hadn't exactly met. I signed, "Do you know Ryker?"

She paused midstep, and an unsure frown touched her face. "Ryker?" she repeated with her voice.

I nodded.

She pressed a finger to her lips for a moment. Like she was unsure about this question. "Did you meet Ryker?" she finally asked after moving her finger from her lips.

I shook my head no. I didn't want to sign in the hallway anymore. I glanced around to see if anyone was watching us, then turned back to her.

"Ryker isn't . . . he's not someone you should be interested in." Even as she said the words, she seemed torn about it. I could see guilt mixed with concern in her eyes. As if she wasn't sure she should be saying this. But it wasn't for selfish reasons she was warning me away. To say I was confused was an understatement.

"He's not always . . . nice," she finally said.

I understood then. She knew he wouldn't accept me when he found out about my being deaf. I was disappointed, but it was an emotion I knew well. I would survive. It was good to know now before I spent too much time thinking about him.

CHAPTER 5

RYKER

Never noticed how little of Hunter I saw at school until I was looking for him. Jesus, did we not pass each other at all? I didn't want to wait until lunch to meet Aurora. I'd also never been this damn anxious to meet a girl in my life. The more I thought about it, the more uncomfortable it made me.

"Did you study for the history test?" Nash asked me, breaking my train of thought.

I shot him a glance. "Yes."

Nash sighed. "I forgot. You got the notes?"

"You don't even have notes?" I asked, not surprised.

He shrugged. "Can't find them. I had some, but I think I left them at Tallulah's."

"Yeah, I've got the notes. They're in the notebook on top of all the other shit in my locker. You know the combination."

"Thanks. Maybe I have enough time to pass this thing," he said. "Tallulah is preoccupied with Hunter's sister. I didn't want to bother her with it or admit that I hadn't studied."

Hunter's sister. That got my attention. "She's met Hunter's sister?" I asked, turning to him.

Nash nodded. "Yeah, they got here about the same time we did. You meet her?"

"Tallulah likes her?" I continued to question him instead of answering him. Tallulah wasn't one to befriend someone easily. She was more reserved. She was careful who she let get close. To say Tallulah wasn't social was an understatement.

"Why wouldn't she? Besides, she noticed Hunter being stressed showing her around today and thought she might need to step in. She's good about paying attention to things like that." You could hear the pride in his voice as he spoke about her.

If I wasn't so damn focused on Aurora, I'd roll my eyes.

"Do you know where they are now?" I asked him, not wanting to talk about Tallulah.

He shrugged. "I would assume headed to Aurora's next period. Or Tallulah has taken her to the library for a break."

Why would she want to go to the library? Was she into

books? How did he know if she was? Why wasn't he giving me more answers, dammit? "How do you know she reads? Did you talk to her?"

Nash frowned at me, confused. "You seem real wound up about this." He paused, then began to grin. "Wait . . . are you interested in her?"

He was going to be an asshole now just to piss me off. I wouldn't be getting shit out of him. My glare only made him laugh before he walked away. I'd have to wait until lunch to find her, that is if we had the same lunch period. Frustrated, I continued to my next class with a scowl on my face. My name was called out twice, but I ignored it, keeping my eyes open for any sign of her.

After an entire morning of wanting to meet this girl, I might not like her at all once I got a chance to speak to her. Which would suck. Because she was the most excitement I'd had at school this year. This building her up to be something was probably going to slap me in the face. Maybe this was just all the Nova bullshit that had bothered me. If I had slept with Nova, this might not be happening. Or it could be. I didn't know. I wasn't even making sense to myself anymore.

Turning the corner, I was almost plowed down by Hunter, who had a serious concerned frown. Not like him at all. The guy was normally very even keel.

"Sorry, Ryker," he said without stopping.

"You okay?" I asked him, wanting to get to the subject of his sister.

He paused and turned back to me. "Just need to get to class. Make sure Aurora"—he paused and added—"my sister, got there."

He was about to start moving again, so I quickly told him, "Tallulah won't let her get lost. She's in good hands."

He sighed then, and the tense way he was holding his shoulders eased some. "So you saw them? She's still with Tallulah?"

"No, but I saw Nash, and he told me Tallulah was showing her around. She won't lose her or leave her side."

He seemed a little relieved but not sure he was going to trust that completely. "She's not good with new people. I need to get to class and make sure she's there," Hunter said, then almost broke into a run getting down the hall. I glanced in the direction of my next class then back at Hunter. Following him would probably get me in trouble for being late twice today.

I also didn't want to meet her with Hunter breathing down her neck. It was weird he was so protective. What was the deal with that? She wasn't a kid. I headed for my class, but the reasons why Hunter was so concerned about Aurora didn't seem normal. They were twins. Shouldn't they fight and get annoyed with each other and shit?

"Is this how it's going to be? You're not even going to try and get my attention?" Nova asked, causing me to pause and glance around for her. I hadn't noticed her, but then I hadn't been looking, either. My head was somewhere else.

She was wearing red. She looked good in it. Nova would look good in about anything she wore. Red, however, was a color she stood out in. "Hey," I said, not sure what else I needed to say. Before I'd laid eyes on Aurora, I'd had plenty to say to Nova. Those things seemed to be put on pause for the moment, though.

She placed a hand on her left hip and slightly cocked her body. The flash of challenge in her eyes was intriguing. She wasn't going to let this go. No guy would walk over her, and she scared me just a little. The intensity. I doubted she was used to guys turning down her offer of sex.

"You've walked past me three times today and said nothing. Not even a glance in my direction. And I know I'm hard to miss." That last comment could be considered confident or cocky. To some it might be sexy. I wasn't sure I liked it, though.

"I didn't notice you," I said, thinking she needed a little hit on that ego of hers. "But I wasn't looking."

She smirked at me. As if I had started a game she knew she was going to win. I stood there waiting for her to say something, but I was running out of time. The late bell was about to ring. When she just kept smirking, I gave a nod and began heading toward my class, hoping I got there before the bell sounded.

"I'll win," Nova called out.

I reached the classroom door and opened it before glancing back at her. Still standing where I had left her. "What?" I asked, confused by that statement.

"This game. I will win."

What the hell was she talking about? What game? The bell sounded, and I stepped into the room without looking back. There was a good chance Nova might be batshit.

I Was Afraid I Would Have to Beg

CHAPTER 6

AURORA

Today hadn't been as awful as I'd imagined. It hadn't been bad at all, really. Except Hunter had been a little over-bearing. I'd asked him to let me meet him in the lunch-room, because I wanted to go to the restroom, and I didn't want him standing guard at the door. I needed a breather. Tallulah had given me a brief one, but Hunter had shown up and taken back being my guardian. Sighing, I looked at myself in the mirror and tried to understand that he had a need to protect me. He always had. He'd been the perfect twin—the beautiful, athletic, hearing child—and I knew he felt guilty about it. He had no reason to, but he did. That was just Hunter.

I couldn't take too long or he'd come looking for me. After running my fingers through my hair, I quickly washed my hands, then headed back to the hallway. I didn't want to face the cafeteria. I'd rather have taken Tallulah up on her offer to show me the library and hide out there with a book. The hallway was empty. I'd stayed in the restroom long enough. This morning it had all looked intimidating. But now, looking down the hallway, I felt as if I'd conquered something and won, even if the day wasn't over yet.

When I turned right to head toward the cafeteria, I froze, startled to see I wasn't alone. My hand had gone to my mouth to cover any sound I may have made. My eyes locked on the guy from this morning. The pounding of my heart slowed some but not much. I was alone with him. What did I do with that? I had wanted to see him again, but not like this. Tallulah hadn't said it, but I knew she hadn't thought Ryker would be okay with my being deaf.

"Hey, I didn't mean to startle you," he said slow enough for me to read his lips. There was a slight frown between his eyes, but also a soft smile was creeping up on his mouth. He seemed confused. I wondered if he'd said something to alert me he was there when my back had been turned.

I stood there, silent. Using my voice with him was not going to happen.

"I'm Ryker," he said when I said nothing. "I saw you this morning."

I nodded and gave him a smile.

He looked unsure of my silence. He obviously hadn't asked about me like I had about him. He didn't realize I couldn't hear and was simply reading his lips. I didn't expect him to ask about me, though. He was beautiful. There had to be a string of girls after him. Hunter said he was with a new girl all the time.

"I'm sorry if I, uh . . . It's just, I saw you this morning and—" He was stumbling over words, or I was having a hard time following along. My silence wasn't helping.

I pointed at my ear and shook my head, then without my voice mouthed, *I'm deaf.*

Slowly his smile faded, and his eyes showed his thoughts so clearly as he took that in. Surprise, then a touch of sadness, then pity. That one always annoyed me. There was no reason to pity someone who was different.

"I'm sorry," he said slowly this time, realizing I had been reading his lips.

Why? I said silently.

His frown deepened, and he studied me. We stood there like that, unaware, for a few moments. It wasn't immediate, but the confusion began to change into understanding. Then a gleam of appreciation shone in his dark eyes. I smiled at him. Proud of me for handling this without help. For not getting flustered or running off. Once I would have. This would have been more than I would have been willing to face. Not now. I had changed.

"It's nice to meet you, Aurora." He said my name. Which meant he *had* asked about me. That simple fact made the smile on my face explode before I could tamp it down. My stomach fluttered with the new knowledge, and I started to say more when a hand wrapped around my upper arm. I knew it was Hunter without turning.

Ryker's eyes left mine to meet my brother's.

Sister was the first word I caught from his lips. I didn't know what else he had said.

I quickly swung my gaze to Ryker, who was talking faster now, and I struggled to follow him. "I know ---- talking ----" was all I got from him, so I turned my focus back to Hunter.

His grip on me tightened slightly, and I jerked away my arm, getting his attention. Signing, I said, "He was being nice. Don't be rude. I am trying to fit in here!"

Hunter's nostrils flared, and he cut his eyes at Ryker then back to me. Then he signed, "He isn't a guy you need to know. He is a player. He uses girls."

Rolling my eyes, I turned back to Ryker. *I'm sorry,* I told him silently, wishing I was brave enough to use my voice.

He shook his head slightly. "It's okay. I understand."

That was it. The look. He understood I was different, and he needed to stay away. Thanks to Hunter, he would. The moment when it was just us out here in the hallway alone was gone. I wouldn't get that again, or the giddy feeling that came with it.

Angry, I watched as he said something to Hunter, then walked away. No good-bye. Nothing. It was over that quickly.

I glared at Hunter. "I'm not hungry. I'll be in the library," I signed, then turned and fled before he could stop me. I needed space and solitude.

Hunter let me go. For that I was thankful. Because I wanted to yell at him and hit his chest a few times.

Carrying my frustrated and angry mix of emotions with me, I found the library, picked up the first book that I came to in the fiction section, then sat down to read. Escape into another world where I wasn't the deaf girl, and hoping it would get my mind off what Hunter had just done. He didn't even realize how humiliating this was.

Before I got through the first chapter, a hand touched my shoulder, and I jumped slightly. I looked up, and my eyes widened at the sight of Ryker. He didn't say anything but handed me a piece of paper. I glanced down at the paper then back at him. His eyes were striking. Hard to look away from. "Read this? Please?" he said slowly.

I reached up and took the paper from his hand. It was torn out of a notebook. His neat handwriting made me wonder if he wrote this clear all the time, or if this was just for my sake.

I'm sorry about earlier. I wasn't prepared for Hunter to be angry about me talking to you. Not sure what he said about me but it is probably true. You can take his advice or you can put my number in your phone and text me. Anytime.

His number was written clearly underneath. I didn't look up at him as I unzipped my book bag, took out my phone, saved his number into my contacts, then sent a simple text.

I think I want to make up my own mind about you.

That was brave. I was proud of myself.

Ryker grinned and replied via text.

Thank God. I was afraid I would have to beg. This way I look much cooler.

I pressed my lips together to keep from laughing. Then tipped my head back to meet his gaze. We stayed there a moment, and the smile on his face was so genuine and almost excited that I found it hard to believe all these warnings I'd been given about him. He didn't seem to care about my being deaf. If he was a player, then why would he go out of his way to get to know me? What I was being told and the guy in front of me didn't add up.

A slight frown interrupted our locked gaze, and he began texting again.

Bell just rang. I'd walk you to your next class but I'm not sure Hunter could handle that just yet. He seems to need time to adjust to you being here.

I nodded and said *okay* silently.

The left corner of his mouth lifted, and there was the slightest dimple in his cheek. I had the urge to touch it. I didn't, but I fantasized about it. "Thanks for your number," he said, still not leaving.

I simply nodded.

Then he winked before turning to go. I sat there, smiling like an idiot and watching him. Once he got to the door, he glanced back and caught me still looking at him. My cheeks flushed from embarrassment. With a slight lift of his head and a pleased look on his face he left the library. I looked back down at my phone to reread our short text conversation. It wasn't much, but I read it over and over until Hunter arrived, telling me to hurry or we would be late for class.

She Drew Me In with Silence
CHAPTER 7

RYKER

I didn't listen to anything during the next two classes. My head was trying to wrap itself around Aurora. Was I that interested in her? Just from her smile? How could I even date her if we couldn't talk? Not normally at least.

But, damn, when she'd been sitting there staring up at me with those big green eyes, I just hadn't cared about anything other than getting to know her more. She drew me in with silence, and it was impressive and scary as hell. How did she have that power with the obvious innocence in her expression? I'd never been attracted to innocence. In fact, I had run from it in the past. Every. Damn. Time.

Then add my lack of compassion to that, and this

seemed like a very bad idea. I had worried about only myself most of my life. Which had been a big, easy ride until Nash had gotten hurt. I did care about that. Nash was my cousin, but we were as close as brothers. Nash being hurt had changed me. I wasn't the same jerk I had been, but I wasn't a Boy Scout, either. Nash's accident had been my wake-up call that life could change in an instant. Getting to know Tallulah had also taught me how shallow I had been. Just last year Tallulah had been overweight, and I had never paid her any attention except to make a joke at her expense. I wasn't proud of that, and if I let myself think about it too much, I felt like shit. I wasn't that guy now. Tallulah hadn't just saved my cousin; she'd forgiven me, too. Even when I didn't deserve it. That kind of generosity is humbling. It makes you think before you speak. I wasn't perfect, and shit still flew out of my mouth at times, but I was better. I just wasn't sure if I had changed enough to pursue someone like Aurora.

Nova was what I was used to. She was fun, exciting, sexy, and knew the rules. She wasn't trying to fall in love and look at me like Tallulah and Nash looked at each other. Nova knew the Ryker I had been, and she didn't care. She wasn't someone I had to work to impress. I didn't have to win her brother over to date her. She was the obvious choice. Made sense to date Nova. Except her eyes didn't make me feel like I'd been slapped in the chest so hard I couldn't catch my breath. Her smile didn't make me want to do everything I could to keep it in place. Nova didn't make me feel . . . this . . . this . . . insanity.

The rest of the day I looked for Aurora but didn't see her. During practice, I found myself watching Hunter and listening to him in case he said something about his sister. I was curious. I wanted to know more about her. Anything really. If he'd just talk about her, I'd be happy. I understood his odd protectiveness over her now. I didn't blame him. She was stunning and sweet, which was a rare combination. If she was my sister . . . no. I wasn't going to even think about that.

Hunter was, per usual at practice, focused on the plays, his passing game, and winning. I'd never seen a more driven athlete. He was the reason we hadn't struggled after our former quarterback, Brady Higgens, graduated. Nash had been working with the freshman quarterback, Kip. He had a shitload of natural talent. Hunter saw it like the rest of us. Because of it, Hunter had gotten even more intense. He had something to prove, and it only helped the team. Hunter truly seemed to love the game.

I loved football too, but I wasn't as intense as Hunter. It was his number one concern in life. I could get distracted, unlike Hunter. I had a hard time focusing, due to Aurora. I doubted that Hunter had ever been distracted from the game by a girl. Which made me wonder just how much of an ass his father was. My dad put a lot of importance on the game, because it would send me to college. I didn't think that was the case with Hunter's dad. It was more, or at least that is how it looked to everyone else.

When I was finally at home and alone in my room, I smiled as I lay back on my bed and started a text to Aurora. I'd debated all afternoon if I should text her tonight. Although the entire time I was arguing with myself about it I knew I was going to. I had dropped two passes and not given a shit about it. My focus had been Aurora.

How was the rest of your day?

I sent the text, smiling like an idiot. I was glad no one was around to witness this. It was late enough that dinner was probably finished at her house. We'd just eaten burgers Mom had picked up on the way home from work. I'd had mine in the living room with Dad while we watched ESPN. Neither of us was in the mood to talk. Mom was in the kitchen on the phone with my aunt in Dallas, Texas. She was about to marry husband number three, and my mother wasn't happy about it.

Nahla, my eleven-year-old sister, sat on the end of the sofa, barely eating her food because she was taking selfies and keeping up her streaks on Snapchat. Unless Mom took her phone away and forced us to eat at the table together, this was the norm. The nights we had to do the family-time thing were rare. My phone dinged, and with it my heart rate increased. She had texted me back.

It was okay. Adjusting will take a while.

Her response concerned me some. She couldn't hear. It made her different, and I knew what dumbasses there were in our school who wouldn't know how to deal with someone unlike themselves. I had once been a dumbass. If she didn't adjust, would she leave? Go somewhere else? Move? I didn't like any of those options.

I looked for you the rest of the day but our paths didn't cross again. Did you see Tallulah anymore?

That I was hoping for. Tallulah would be great at helping her adjust. She'd also be a good friend. And I wanted Aurora to like it here. The reasons, I admit, were selfish, but I didn't like the idea of her leaving.

Yes. She saved me from Hunter's hovering again. I know he means well but he was more nervous than I was.

That was a short text for the long period of time the "..." from her typing appeared on the screen. I wondered if she had said more, then deleted it. If she had, what was it she had decided not to say. Damn, why was I getting so worked up over texting? I needed to calm the hell down.

Brothers are protective. It's what we do. My little sister is a brat. I couldn't imagine having her at school with me.

Nahla wasn't boy crazy yet. I knew the day was coming soon, and I dreaded it. I liked her little. I could deal with the stupid-ass Disney shows she watched or the cotton-candy body spray she used that stunk up the entire upstairs, not just the bathroom. I wasn't ready for her to date. I doubted I ever would be. Even when she was old enough.

I got used to my independence at my old school. Not needing Hunter. Being able to manage on my own. I want that here too. Getting him to understand it is hard though.

I thought about that and reread it several times. She was seventeen. She wasn't eleven. She should get to drive her own car and live like the rest of us. Being treated differently after having a life where she had been equal to the others had to be hard. Again, the fear she'd leave and find another school like the one she had left scared me. Time. She needed time to like it here. I would do all I could to help her fit in.

Give it time. Hunter should chill out. Relax when he sees you adjusting. Making friends. Finding your own way. How do you think he's going to react to you dating?

I erased and rewrote that last question three times before hitting send and literally holding my breath. From watching Hunter today, I didn't imagine he was going to be too fond of her dating anyone. Especially me. My reputation wasn't that great. I knew it was going to be a hurdle, but I was willing to get over it. Hell, Hunter could come too. We could double-date like we were in junior high again. I was fine with it if it meant I got to be around her more. Amazing how she made me okay with things I would have made fun of just this morning.

I've been dating awhile now. My boyfriend, Denver, is back in North Carolina though. I don't think there will be much dating here with him being so far away.

Boyfriend. Denver? What kind of name was Denver? It was a fucking city in Colorado. The idea of this Denver pissed me off. It shouldn't surprise me. Aurora was beautiful, her smile was addicting, and she was sweet. Why wouldn't she have a boyfriend? But why mention it now? Why not earlier when it was clear I'd been flirting. A million things ran through my mind as I stared at her words, trying to decide what to say or if I should just stop texting.

But there was one simple fact.

Denver wasn't here.

I was.

Long distance relationships can suck.

There, I said it. Now for her to respond. If she came back with their love was too strong for distance to break, I'd back out. Maybe. Probably not. Who was I kidding? Denver was going down. He was miles away.

I know. I'm waiting for the text where he breaks it off. I'm prepared for it and a bit surprised he didn't do it before I left.

Better response than I could have hoped for. Denver needed to prepare himself and get ready for his own text. Because if I had my way, Aurora would be the one sending the breakup text. Grinning, I texted.

He'd be an idiot.

There was a long pause, several minutes, before she replied simply.

Thank you.

*I Had to Wonder if Any of Them
Knew Ryker at All*

CHAPTER 8

AURORA

Hunter touched my shoulder as I was buttering my waffle, and I looked up at him.

"Why are you smiling?" he asked, his brow wrinkled with his frown. As if he was trying to read my mind. Last time I checked, he wasn't a telepath.

I shrugged, not realizing I had been smiling but not surprised, either. I knew what my thoughts were, and they were happy ones.

"I like waffles," I said, using my voice.

"They're frozen from a box. That's nothing to get that excited about." He said the words as he signed.

I shrugged again and went back to buttering my waffle,

trying not to smile. It was hard, though. I'd texted with Ryker Lee until I fell asleep around midnight. I had never done that before. It had been exciting. When I had told him about Denver, I expected him to stop texting me. I almost hadn't told him. But the guilt of not being honest was too much. If Ryker was thinking of asking me out, he needed to know about Denver. I would have broken up with Denver if he had asked. I didn't want to admit that, but I knew I would have. Now that he knew about Denver, I had to face the fact he might not ask me out. My smile had faded on its own. Those thoughts weren't happy ones. But after I had told him about Denver, he had continued to text me. For hours.

Instead of it pushing me away, he seemed to not care at all. It was very confident of him. One could also say cocky, but I didn't think it fit him. After all the warnings I had been given about him, I had to wonder if any of them knew Ryker at all. The guy I had gotten to know last night in the texts wasn't anything like he'd been described to me. He'd been sweet and funny and listened to me. He cared about my life back home, my favorite food, my favorite books . . .

Another tap on my shoulder.

I took a bite of my waffle before looking at Hunter again. He was still frowning. "You're doing it again. The smiling."

I chewed my food and scowled at my brother. He was

being ridiculous. Why couldn't I smile? Wasn't it better that I smiled? What if I had been crying in my room, wanting to go back to North Carolina? Shouldn't my smiling make him happy? Once I swallowed, I replied, "I slept well. I'm not nervous about school. I'm happy. Is that okay?" using my voice again.

He sighed a little too dramatically and grabbed two frozen waffles from the box I hadn't returned to the freezer yet. Then he went to stick them in the toaster. I continued eating mine, wishing we had syrup. There was not a lot of sugar or sweet things in this house. Our stepmother, Ella, was a yoga instructor and very into healthy eating. Everything was organic. Except these waffles. Ella was at the gym by six in the morning with her first class. So she had no time to make us breakfast, and even if she could, I doubted she would. Buying the waffles was something she had to accept. It was Hunter's choice for breakfast, and I was good with it too. I wouldn't mind some Frosted Flakes, but Hunter said I'd be lucky if I pulled that one off. Even if I did convince her to buy the cereal, I would have to then convince her to buy real milk, because the almond milk in the fridge was disgusting. I'd tried it yesterday morning and had to spit it in the sink. When I had turned back around after wiping my mouth, I caught Hunter laughing at me.

I turned to look at Hunter, and sure enough, he was watching me still.

"What does Dad eat for breakfast?" I asked him, realizing Dad was always gone when we got up in the morning.

"Good ol' Jack's biscuits with sausage and cheese. Ella doesn't know, or she'd freak out," he said with a smirk.

I laughed. Ella was young. Much younger than Mom. I hadn't asked, but I would guess she wasn't thirty yet. Which was a bit weird, seeing as Dad was forty-two. But whatever. She made him happy. Even if he had to sneak off to eat good food.

"You like Tallulah, then?" he asked me, changing the subject back to school things.

I nodded. "She's nice. Not what I expected when I first saw her."

"She hasn't always looked like that," he replied.

I wasn't sure what that meant, but before I could ask for clarification, he glanced at the clock on the oven. "We need to go."

I finished off my waffle and took a drink of the freshly squeezed orange juice Ella had made with the fancy juicer sitting on the counter last night. She had offered to juice me some vegetables and fruit for my breakfast this morning. I almost gagged at the thought, but managed to shake my head and mouth, *No thank you.* Ella didn't sign. And

I wasn't comfortable enough around her to use my voice.

I'd had to divert my gaze from Hunter, who was covering his mouth to keep from laughing at her offer. I would start laughing too if I looked at him. That was one of the things that hadn't changed with our living apart. We shared emotions very easily. When he was happy, it made me happy. When he was sad, I felt it too. Before I even saw him. I just knew. It was a unique bond.

I picked up my backpack and followed Hunter outside to his truck. I never imagined Hunter as one to drive a truck. He had always talked about how he wanted a Mustang when he turned sixteen. He had posters of Mustangs through the years all over his room before he moved away. The large F-150 he drove was nothing like a Mustang. I hadn't asked him about it, but from what I saw in the school parking lot, it seemed to fit in better than a Mustang would.

My phone vibrated, and I felt a tingle of excitement. Once I was seated in the passenger seat and buckled, I pulled it out, hoping to see Ryker's name. But it wasn't.

It was Mom's.

With a touch of my finger I reluctantly opened her text. I missed her. Even after the way she'd left and the yelling between her and Hunter. I missed her. I wished I'd said I had loved her when she left. But I had just stood there. Watching her go with not even a good-bye. Hunter's emotional pain had intensified mine and vice versa.

Good morning my favorite girl in the world. I hope you had a good day at school yesterday. I thought about you often.

Mom wasn't a bad mother. She had always loved me. She'd sacrificed a lot for me. Dad had left her, and she had still loved him. I could see it, and I hurt for her. Now she had found Lou, and he made her happy. It was time she got to be happy again. I'd seen her sad for far too long.

Good morning. School wasn't at all like I expected. I made a couple friends. I'm going to be okay here.

I knew she needed to hear that. I wanted to add that I loved her. But I also wanted to apologize for letting her leave without saying the words and hugging her. I realized the truck had stopped, and lifted my head to see Hunter staring at me. "Who is it?" he asked, frowning again.

"Mom," I said simply. He snarled. He didn't agree with me about Mom. I wasn't sure why, but he blamed her for the divorce. For letting him leave with Dad. It was almost as if he had wanted her to fight for him to stay. I didn't understand that completely.

"She just now remembering to check on you? How thoughtful." Although I couldn't hear him, I knew those words were laced with sarcasm. He turned his attention back to the road, and the truck began moving again.

That's wonderful news. I knew you would fit in. You're smart, beautiful, and kind. People are drawn to you. I love you. And I am here. Text me often. I miss you.

I felt tears unexpectedly sting my eyes. I missed her too. She was so far away now. Even if she had been a bit withdrawn and unhappy the past four years, she was mine. And I loved her.

I love you too.

I sent the text and felt relief as I did. I wanted her to know I did love her. And I understood her at least a little.

I didn't look at Hunter the rest of the drive to school. If I couldn't see him, he couldn't say anything to me I didn't want to hear. My chest ached a little at the moment, and I needed to get myself composed. Thinking about Mom was hard.

She's Innocent, She's Sheltered,
She's the Quarterback's Sister,
and She Is Deaf

CHAPTER 9

RYKER

Getting through breakfast and to school without breaking down and texting Aurora was difficult. But I'd been the last one to text last night. I knew she'd probably fallen asleep, but still, it was her turn. If I came across as too needy, it could send her running in the other direction. Girls needed some mystery. At least that was what I had heard once . . . in a movie, I think. Who knew how accurate it was? I could just text her. Stop waiting for her to text me and driving myself crazy.

Glancing at my phone for the twentieth time since I woke up, I growled in frustration. Still nothing from Aurora. I knew she was here. I'd looked for Hunter's truck the moment I pulled in the parking lot. Hell, I had even gotten to school ten minutes early, and he'd still beat me here. I had tried to arrive when they did so I'd have a chance to see her. Maybe walk inside with her.

I wondered if she'd mentioned our texting to Hunter this morning. Hunter and I got along fine on the field. But we weren't tight. I hadn't grown up with him. My closest friend other than my cousin Nash was Asa. The others in our group had graduated and moved on to college this year. It was different playing ball without them. I'd been so excited over this being my senior year, I hadn't expected the void I'd feel with the guys I'd always played on the field with being gone. Adjusting to Hunter as quarterback had been easy enough. However, he hadn't been real happy about me talking to Aurora yesterday. If he had said something to her to make her stop this before I even got a chance, I could possibly be screwed.

Stepping inside the school, I admittedly scanned the halls for Aurora. Turning the corner down the south hall, I found Nova instead. She'd texted me last night, and I had forgotten about it until now. Seeing her reminded me. I hadn't responded because I'd been too busy in my conversation with Aurora. I also hadn't responded because I wasn't going to encourage her. Not that she needed any encouragement. She was determined.

"I don't like games," she said in a saucy tone. "Maybe some games, but not the one you seem to want to play."

Just yesterday she was saying she would win this game. I wasn't playing a game, nor did I want to play a game with her. It was time for her to let it go and move on. We had flirted with the idea of sex. Nothing more. I had changed my mind on that before Aurora. Why was she pushing this so hard?

"I was already in bed when you texted me last night. Sorry I didn't respond." That was the truth. I felt better about myself already for not lying. Normally I'd make up some bullshit so she would smile and go about her business.

She puckered her lips in the seductive way she often did in the photos she posted of herself on Instagram. It looked good on her. She had great lips, but it was doing nothing for me.

"And this morning when you woke up? You couldn't respond then?"

Here I could lie or be honest. I was thinking Aurora could have done the same thing. Texted me back. Said *good morning* or something. Damn, I was acting like a girl.

"I could have. But I didn't. I was trying to get to school on time." Not for reasons she may assume, though.

Nova sighed, rolling her shoulders back to make sure

her chest was at its best viewing advantage. I knew that move. I'd seen many girls do it. "I'm not going to keep wasting my time with you, Ryker. If you're interested, you make the next move." She then spun around and walked away with a swish in her hips I barely glanced at. Nova was drama, but at least this meant the game she was accusing me of playing was over.

Glancing away from Nova, my eyes instantly met Aurora's. She was standing at a locker with her hand on it as if she were closing it. Her focus, though, was completely on me. Had she been there all along? I replayed the scene with Nova, and although Aurora couldn't hear what was being said, I wondered if she had read my lips. Nova's back had been to her, so she couldn't have read her lips. I didn't waste time thinking more about it. My standing here and looking at her wasn't helping.

I made my way through the crowded hallway to get to her. I hadn't looked for Hunter, but as I approached Aurora, I realized he had to be near. And I wasn't sure if he knew we'd spoken or texted yesterday. Since I had heard nothing from her today.

She smiled as I finally reached her.

"Hey," I said, staring into those eyes again, realizing my memory hadn't exaggerated how incredible they were.

Hello, she said silently. I liked watching her lips. The soft pink gloss on them made me think of other things I'd like to do to her lips. I felt a little guilty when the thought of biting her bottom lip came to mind.

"What class do you have first?" I asked, slower than normal.

"She's got Lit. Why?" Hunter asked as his hand wrapped around her upper arm. Aurora tensed up, and I saw her inhale sharply and shoot her brother a warning glare. It was too damn cute to be intimidating.

"I wanted to walk her there," I told him in the nicest tone I had. Normally I'd respond differently to a guy talking to me like he had, but this was real damn important.

"I can handle it. I'm going there too. You aren't." He said the last bit with such protective emphasis I realized this was going to be harder than I'd thought. I also didn't think Aurora had mentioned our texting to him.

"No, I'm not going in that direction," I agreed, and turned my focus back to Aurora. "I just wanted a chance to talk to her before the day started."

Her eyes smiled before her lips did. She was good at reading my lips. I liked that.

"She can't talk to you." Hunter said that as if she was broken. I didn't like it. I suddenly didn't give a fuck if he was her brother. I swung my now-annoyed gaze to him.

"She communicates just fine with me." I made sure to keep my mouth in clear view of Aurora so she would know what I was saying.

She was between us now. Her back to me as she looked up at Hunter. She began signing, and I hadn't seen her do it before. But watching her hands, I noticed they were dainty, with light pink polish on her nails. She wore a small sapphire ring on her right middle finger. Hands had never been something I'd noticed before, but damn if hers weren't perfect. Like the rest of her. I wished like hell I could sign. She communicated that way so easily. She didn't have to struggle to talk or read lips. I wanted her to feel that comfortable talking to me.

"I'm not dealing with this now. We're going to be late. Come on," Hunter said, and he took her arm again, which was starting to really piss me the hell off. She wasn't a child he had to drag around. She stumbled as she went with him and turned her head to gaze back at me.

She didn't have to say anything. The embarrassment and apology in her eyes made my stomach twist. I didn't like knowing she was upset and I had had something to do with it. When she finally got her footing, I saw her jerk her arm free from Hunter, pull her blue-and-white book bag up on her shoulder, and storm away from him, walking faster and putting distance between them.

That bit of attitude made me grin. I was glad to see she wasn't letting him control her. She had spunk.

"What are you doing?" Nash's tone was a mixture of disbelief and annoyance. "Dude, we are about to be in the playoffs. Messing with the quarterback's head is a fucking terrible idea. I can't play anymore, so I can't get out there and save your ass on the field."

I watched until Aurora turned to go into her room, and, like I had hoped, she paused and glanced back at me. I hadn't moved. She saw it, and she smiled. Damn.

"Shit," Nash muttered. He had seen it too. That made me smile even wider.

"She's different," I said finally, looking at my cousin.

"Yeah. She's innocent. She's sheltered. She's the quarterback's sister, and she's deaf." He said the last thing softer, as if saying it was something he regretted.

"She's smart. Really smart. Quick witted. She's thoughtful and honest. Even when it might be something you don't want to hear. She loves pizza with extra sausage. She enjoys reading the classics, *The Great Gatsby* is her favorite, but she also reads mysteries and paranormal. Almond milk makes her gag, and she loves the color pink but won't wear it anywhere but on her nails because of her hair. And she's beautiful." Those were the things I meant when I said she was different.

Nash groaned. "Why? Why does this have to happen now?"

"What?"

Nash looked at me and shook his head in frustration. "You pulling your head out of your ass and seeing a girl for more than a body and a fun time."

"I've never met a girl like her."

Nash studied me a moment, then hung his head. He rubbed his temples before sighing in defeat. "We're fucked. I have been working with Kip, but the kid is not ready to take over in the playoffs if Hunter's head isn't in the game. There goes the championship."

You Were Warned
about My Reputation
CHAPTER 10

AURORA

I didn't mean to upset Hunter.

I glanced down at the text from Ryker after sitting in Literature class fuming for well over twenty minutes. Hunter had stepped way out of line. As soon as this class ended, I was going to get him alone and put down some boundaries. I had gotten so upset I'd gone to full-on signing in the hallway. Something I hadn't ever planned on doing.

Right now that was the least of my concerns, though. Hunter had humiliated me in front of Ryker. He had no right to act the way he did. Ryker had been nice and friendly. I was surprised when I'd glanced back to see him in the hallway where I had been forced to leave him. He was watching me. The look in his eyes hadn't been angry, annoyed, or withdrawn. Which were all things I had feared I'd see. Instead he'd seemed sad. Almost worried. He also looked like he . . . missed me. Which was odd and sweet at the same time.

I waited until the teacher had taken a seat and everyone was busy reading before hiding the phone in my lap and replying.

Hunter was a jerk. He needs to apologize. I'm sorry he acted that way.

I hit send and glanced back at my brother, who was watching me. I glared at him, making sure he knew I was still furious, then turned back to the book in front of me we were supposed to be reading. I couldn't focus on the words in the book. It was pointless to try and read. The scene in the hall kept replaying in my head. I'd seen Ryker talking to the girl, and she'd been upset with him. I could see her body language enough to tell that. He hadn't been real concerned about it, and he'd seemed a bit confused. Too many people had blocked my view, and I hadn't seen his mouth clear enough to know what he was saying. Not that it was my business.

I don't have the best reputation. I should've warned you and I should've expected his reaction. But I'm going to talk to him. I know you have a boyfriend but I'd like to get the chance to know you. To be your friend.

Although that was sweet, it made my heart sink. He wanted to be my friend. It was silly for that to feel like such a letdown. I had told him about Denver. He could just be respecting that. Or he could simply want to be my friend.

The gorgeous girl who he'd had a conversation with in the hall, she'd been confident, turned heads, and seemed to have some kind of relationship with him. The way he'd responded to her and the way she was so worked up said they'd had something before or maybe now. I wondered if she was one of the reasons for his bad reputation. The idea didn't feel good. I pushed all that aside and replied.

I had already heard some of your reputation. Hunter doesn't get to make my decisions for me or determine my friends.

I wanted to add *and I'd like to get to know you, too.* But I wasn't sure if that would make me vulnerable. I didn't know much about Ryker. There seemed to be a lot I should know. A lot that people wanted me to know. But I enjoyed getting to know him organically. Without prior knowledge of him. Or others' opinions. Besides, everything they could tell me would be secondhand information, and I had never cared for or participated in gossip.

It wasn't fair to him. Friends was the best idea. We had only just met yesterday. If we became friends, then I could learn more about him. See if this reputation of his was an issue or not. Wanting more than friendship from him so soon was silly anyway.

You were warned about my reputation? I'm not surprised. But I am a little surprised you gave me a chance so far. I'd think a girl like you wouldn't give someone with my past a chance at . . . friendship.

I smiled at that. Even if I was wrong and that hadn't been meant to sound flirty, it did. I liked it. Much better than the friendship talk. There was a possibility I was naive and I could regret this, but I didn't think I would. He was so nice. Last night I felt like I really got to know him. And he had flirted then, too. I knew flirting. I wasn't imagining that. I wanted him to flirt. Acting like I didn't was just pointless. The truth was the truth.

I like to make my own decisions and form my own opinions.

That was simple. I sent it, then glanced back at the teacher to make sure I wasn't being watched. He was busy on his laptop. I tried to focus on the words I'd already read this year, but my gaze kept going to my phone. Waiting on Ryker's response to my text.

I never got this excited over text messages from Denver, who hadn't texted me at all yesterday. The last time we had talked had been Sunday. It hadn't been very long, either. He'd mostly been checking to see if I had settled in. Asked about my brother and if I was ready to face regular public school. Nothing fun or thrilling.

I realized Denver was comfortable for me. All I knew. I tried to remember if there had been a time when Denver had excited me or given me flutters in my stomach. I didn't think there had been. We had just been good friends who spent a lot of time together. Kissing had been nice but not done very often. We mostly talked about common interests, school, friends we shared, et cetera.

I've not met many people who can say that but you . . . I believe.

I was still smiling down at his response when I saw everyone jump up out of their seats like the place was on fire. Which meant the bell had rung, and they were ready to bolt so they got as much time in the hallways to socialize as possible. That had not been important to me yesterday. However, today I found myself rushing to get my stuff in my bag and out the door like the others.

Hunter stepped in front of me to block my escape, and I sighed as I met his gaze.

"Was that Ryker you were texting during class?"

I gave him a sharp nod and raised my eyebrows to challenge him.

"What about Denver?" he asked, throwing out his own challenge.

I shrugged.

"Are you still with Denver?" he pushed.

I nodded. Then added, *Ryker is a friend. Or could be. He wants to be.* My words were silent, but I knew he read my lips.

He rolled his eyes. "You're being naive."

"Then let me be," I begged.

I jerked my book bag up and stepped around him to get out the door. He'd already wasted enough of my time. I hadn't seen Ryker in the halls much at all yesterday. I doubted today would be different, but I had hopes.

Tallulah and Naz were coming toward me in the hallway when I walked out alone, not checking to see if Hunter was hot on my trail with his overbearing self. Tallulah smiled, and my annoyance faded. It felt nice to know someone and feel as if you had somewhere to fit in. This wasn't how I'd expected it to all happen. I'd thought it would be harder. Painful even. I had imagined tears in my bedroom at night, missing my friends, my security, even my mom.

The reality was much better.

"Good morning. Is today easier?" Tallulah signed.

I glanced back over my shoulder to see Hunter coming up behind me and sighed. Then, turning back to her, I replied, "He's being stubborn." Using hands as well. People seeing me do this didn't seem to bother me so much today. Ryker's attention had made me feel more confident.

Tallulah frowned, then her eyes went to Hunter, and I could tell by her expression he was speaking.

I spun around quickly to catch what he was telling her. All I saw was him say "Ryker." He finished, then purposely didn't meet my eyes. Whatever. I was not arguing with him in the hallway.

I gave him my back and groaned with frustration. Tallulah gave me a sympathetic smile. "Why don't you go with me?" she said slow enough that I could read her lips, not looking at my brother for approval, and I appreciated that more than she could know. She nodded her head for us to go, and I went with her as we walked away from them and toward my next period class.

That's Not a Battle
You're Gonna Win
CHAPTER 11

RYKER

I'd been expecting him. At some point today, I knew Hunter would find me. Had this been last year, I doubted he would have been so bold. But this year he was the quarterback, and with that came a sense of power.

When he called out my name as Nash and I were walking to the cafeteria, Nash paused, and I felt him tense beside me. He had been expecting it too. We hadn't talked about it much, but Nash didn't approve, and I knew it.

"Careful," Nash whispered to me as I turned around to face Hunter. I didn't expect him to throw a punch. He wasn't a physical guy, nor had I seen a temper on the field. Brady Higgins had always been the quarterback I played for until this year. He'd been a much different QB. His temper wasn't something he led with, but we had always known it was there. If this had been him I was dealing with, I would have turned, ready to block a hit.

"Yeah," I replied when I saw the tight line of Hunter's mouth and scowl between his brow. I wasn't sure I'd ever seen Hunter angry, come to think of it. This look was a new one. He should use it on the field.

He stopped a few feet in front of me. If I hadn't been studying him so hard, I would have missed the slight uneasiness in his eyes. His angry expression didn't mask the fact he wasn't as confident as he wanted to be.

"Aurora has a boyfriend" was how he decided to address this. "She's not available."

I gave a small nod. "I know. She told me about Denver," I replied, not missing the way my knowing the boyfriend's name threw him off a little. He was surprised and even more hesitant. But he wasn't going to let this stop him from getting his point across.

"She's sensitive. And she's never met anyone like you before. She trusts too easily. She doesn't understand . . . how you casually do relationships."

Nash was rigid at my side. Not for a second did I think he was about to pounce on Hunter, but he was preparing to stop me if Hunter said the wrong thing. I shot my cousin an amused look and turned my gaze back to Hunter. "I like Aurora. I know she's not available, but if she was, I would never pursue her as a casual fling. She's different."

Hunter's hands balled into fists at his sides, and his eyes flared as he took a step toward me. His face was bloodred. Nash's hand was on my shoulder immediately. He was protecting Hunter. He didn't have to. I was fairly certain that if I hit her brother, then my chances with Aurora were over. Nash didn't understand that, though. He was thinking I might take out the quarterback and get suspended. Did he not listen to anything I had said about Aurora this morning? Or did he just think I was full of BS?

"Don't fucking ever call her different again!" Hunter's tone was laced with threat, fury, and pain. He'd been protecting her for years. I should have chosen my words more carefully. I realized my mistake, and I respected Hunter for the way he immediately went into protective mode. Not caring that I was bigger than him. That Nash was bigger than him.

"She's kind, smart, funny, honest, and real. When I called her different, it was a compliment. I've not met a girl like her before. She makes me smile."

Hunter swallowed hard then. His throat constricted. The way his body was tensed eased some. But he didn't seem to relax completely. He stood there in silence, studying me this time. I was sincere, and I hoped he could see that.

"All she can ever be is your friend and even then . . ." He didn't complete that sentence but turned and walked away. Nothing more. I watched him go, wanting to call out to him and ask him to finish that sentence. For Aurora's sake, I didn't.

Nash let out a long sigh, and his hand left my shoulder. I watched Hunter go, wondering what he had decided not to say. I liked Hunter. But I wasn't sure I would have liked what he had been about to say, and getting him to say it would cause problems.

"You need to let this go," Nash finally said. I looked at my cousin. His frown was one I understood. He was thinking the same thing I had.

"I like her."

Nash nodded. "I know. But . . ." He glanced at the retreating Hunter. "That's not a battle you're gonna win."

"She likes me, too. I make her smile."

Nash ran a hand over his head and groaned. "Why? Why did it have to be her that made you go from player to good guy? Could you not have found someone . . . else? You just met her yesterday. You have texted with her. Talked to her briefly at school. You don't really know her."

I grinned then. He knew as well as I did it didn't work

that way. "When I looked at her the first time, it was like . . . everything made sense."

Nash rolled his eyes. "Great. Now you're a fucking romantic. That's just perfect."

I wasn't trying to be romantic. I was explaining it the best way I could. Aurora was worth whatever obstacles I had to jump through. For now, I was just asking for friendship. I wanted a reason to be near her. To talk to her. It wasn't like I'd asked her on a date.

"Some things are worth the wait and work."

Nash shook his head. "This is more than that. You're ignoring the fact Hunter was too smart to verbalize."

There it was again. The silent warning. The one I wanted to believe was misunderstood. I knew it wasn't uncommon around here. Nash's mom had dealt with the same thing when she started dating my uncle. I'd heard the stories. You'd think people would have moved on from the color of someone's skin, but not in Alabama and definitely not in Lawton.

"I think you're wrong about that," I told Nash. I wanted him to be wrong was what I should have said.

He looked a little angry as he stared down the now almost empty hallway. "I'm not."

"There y'all are." Tallulah's voice stopped me from responding to Nash. We both turned our heads to see

Tallulah and Aurora making their way toward us. They had come from the cafeteria.

"I didn't see y'all go inside," Nash said, stepping toward her to put his arm around her shoulders.

"We got there before the crowd." Tallulah said the words but also signed. I had seen her sign before to Aurora in the hallway. I was jealous that she could communicate with her like that. That class we had in sixth grade where we learned to use basic sign language no longer seemed like a joke to me. I wished I'd paid attention. All I could remember was my name, or most of it. I wasn't sure if I knew the letter *K* anymore.

Aurora finally met my gaze, and she smiled. That made the annoyance with my thoughts fade, and I fought off the urge to walk over and touch her. The way Nash so comfortably touched Tallulah. I envied him that.

"Have you eaten?" I asked her.

She watched my lips closely, then nodded.

"We were in line first. We ate while waiting on the two of you. What have you been doing?" Tallulah used sign as she said all this. Aurora watched her, then turned her eyes back to me.

I felt Nash's gaze on me. He wasn't sure how to respond and was waiting on me. I didn't want to keep things from Aurora. If I intended to earn her trust and convince her

Denver wasn't the guy for her, I had to start now, telling
her the truth.

"Hunter wanted to talk to me," I said the words looking at her, and made sure she could see my lips clearly.

Her eyes widened in concern and a touch of anger as
she lifted them to look at me. *I'm sorry.* She said the words
silently; then, without warning, she turned and walked
quickly away.

I started to go after her, but Tallulah grabbed my arm.
"Don't. This is a fight between her and her brother. Let
her deal with it."

I didn't want to listen to Tallulah. I wanted to have
more time with Aurora. But I knew Tallulah's advice was
probably better than my reaction. Besides, Hunter would
only get more agitated if I showed up.

"She likes you." The way that Tallulah said it, it was
clear she was worried about that. Tallulah had been hurt
once by my words. I had been callous with Tallulah's feelings all my life. She'd only heard me once. I knew I had
said many things over the years about her weight to others. Many times Nash had heard me and scowled at me.
Even corrected me. I felt guilt when I thought about not
only Tallulah but the others at whose expense I'd gotten a
laugh. Getting to know Tallulah was like having a bucket of
cold water dumped over me this year. She'd finally been the

one to teach me how painful words could be and that they could be forgiven but not forgotten. I was different now. I didn't make fun of others. I wasn't out there trying to be their best friend, but I tried to consider them more often. Tallulah had seen me change. At least I thought she had, but she still was worried about Aurora's interest in me.

"She also knows Nash's name now," Tallulah added with a lighter tone. "Until I signed it to her during lunch when talking about y'all, she had thought it was Naz. I kinda like Naz."

I glanced over at Tallulah smirking at Nash, who just chuckled. "I'm not a fan personally," he was teasing her, and at that moment they were in their own little world.

It Had Been the Last Time
I Ordered a Chocolate Milkshake

CHAPTER 12

AURORA

I was surprised to see my dad waiting on me after school. Yesterday Hunter had taken me home, but he'd had to leave football practice to do it. Dad hadn't been happy about that when the coach had called last night to discuss Hunter's leaving early.

Ella was supposed to pick me up after school from now on. I'd walked outside looking for her red convertible BMW to find my dad in his silver Navigator instead. Not having to see Hunter until this evening was a relief. It was weird to be so angry with my brother. I didn't like this feeling, but it was his fault.

I opened the passenger-side door and climbed inside.

Then turned to Dad to sign, "This is a surprise."

He grinned and leaned over to kiss my temple. "A good one, I hope," he replied, signing.

I nodded, returning his smile.

He followed the line of cars out of the pickup area while I buckled my seat belt. I was old enough to drive, but until now I hadn't wanted to. It scared me. I knew being deaf didn't mean I couldn't drive a car. It was simply fear of it that had kept me from even learning. Dad had asked me about it on Sunday. I'd told him that I didn't want to. However, as I watched others walk out to their cars and climb inside, I wondered if I was making it into something much harder than it was.

Dad didn't turn in the direction of home when he left the parking lot. Instead he went toward town. I glanced at him, and he shot me a wink. I couldn't ask him where we were going while he was driving because I wouldn't be able to read his lips while he looked straight ahead. I leaned back and watched instead. I hoped we weren't going to the gym to see Ella. I liked her, but she was nervous around me. It was an adjustment for all of us.

When he pulled into Sonic and parked at one of the ordering spots, he turned to me. "What do you want?"

I remembered him bringing us here four years ago. The last time he had brought us to a Sonic after school was to tell us he and mom were getting a divorce. I'd cried. Not a memory I wanted to think about it.

It had been the last time I ordered a chocolate milkshake.

"Are we here because you're going to tell me bad news?" I asked, not feeling very hungry.

He frowned a moment; then I saw when he, too, remembered the last time we'd had an after-school Sonic milkshake together. The apologetic look in his eyes was easy enough to read. I hadn't wanted to make him feel bad.

I wasn't going to be able to order anything until I knew why we were here. "Why did you bring me here, then?"

He inhaled deeply then exhaled, as if he needed a moment to think about what he was going to say. I waited, getting more nervous by the second. All kinds of things ran through my head.

"I want to talk to you about the cochlear implant. I know you are against it, but I think it's time to have you evaluated again—"

I cut him off. "No," I said, using my voice. The way his eyes widened, I must have used it loudly. I didn't want to talk about that. I had been to the meetings with doctors. I'd heard the good and the bad. In my former school I had seen both success and failure with the procedure among other students there. I was not willing to try. It terrified me. I'd told my mother as much after talking to the doctors about it. She'd let it go. Let me make my own decision.

"Honey," he began, and I shook my head no. It made me angry. I could see in his eyes he thought he knew what was best for me. He'd left me four years ago. He didn't know me that well anymore. Yet he thought he knew what I needed. He had always controlled and molded Hunter into the football player he wanted him to be. Hunter let him. I wasn't Hunter. No one was going to control me. No one was going to make me what they wanted me to be.

"Don't. You weren't at the meetings. You don't know what they all told me." I wasn't an ideal candidate for an implant. They had reluctantly told Mom and me that. Then they'd told me what the best results I could expect were and the very possible side effects that could come with it. There was too much against me. I wasn't going through all that. The idea had sounded good at first, but then I began thinking of the negative side effects and the fear of my world completely changing. I was happy the way I was. I didn't want to try and change it.

"You would have a normal life. One that you don't even know you're missing," he began again. He was giving me the look he gave Hunter when telling him how to live his life. I knew it well. Fear gripped me. I didn't want to be pushed or forced into this. I'd researched it. I wanted no part of it.

"I said NO!" I was more than likely yelling. The force behind my panic that he could actually make me do this came through strong.

Dad sat there a moment in silence. His jaw clenched. I waited for him to say more, when all I wanted to do was get away from him. The controlling way he led others in his life had never touched me. I'd witnessed it though. My mother had been kept under his thumb most of my life. It surprised me that Ella got away with what she did, and I wondered how long that would last until he started controlling her, too. While I sat there, getting worked up about all of this, I saw his shoulders relax, and then finally he sighed. "Okay," he said, looking at me. It wasn't going to be this easy. I knew that. He was just done arguing for now. That didn't make me feel better. It was my body. Not his. Did he want another perfect child like Hunter? Was that it? I was living with him now, and working around my being deaf was too hard on him?

The longer I stared at the menu the angrier I got. Jerking open the passenger-side door, I jumped down out of the Navigator. I didn't glance back at him. It was the same as ignoring him. He couldn't say anything to me if I wasn't looking at him. And I called that a blessing. At least in times like these.

I did glance both ways to check for any moving vehicles

before storming off across the parking lot. I wasn't sure where I was going, but I needed distance. I didn't want to be in the car with him. I didn't want to be in his house, either. If he couldn't accept me the way I was, then I wanted to leave. If only I had somewhere to go. My old home was no longer. My mother wasn't offering to take me in. This was all I had.

I had to turn sideways to slip between two cars parked too closely together, then made it to the grassy patch on the other side. If I followed the road, it would lead back to the school. I could go there and wait until Hunter was done with practice. Then I'd have to explain all this, and I wasn't in the mood. I was more concerned with what he was going to say to Ryker.

Home was a couple of miles farther away. Walking that far wasn't appealing, but better than getting back in my dad's car.

Speaking of my dad's car, it was slowing to a stop beside me. I wanted to glare at it. At him. But I kept walking. Realizing it was very unlikely he was going to let me walk down the side of the road. Mom would have. She'd have been mad at me for getting out of the car during a conversation. Dad wasn't like Mom. He was overprotective. I'd forgotten about that.

He was also probably calling my name, as if that would

do any good. At that thought I felt a little sorry for him. This was new for him. He was adjusting just like I was. I paused. Sighed. Then turned to him.

"Get in the car" was very clearly read on his lips.

He looked frustrated, even a little angry.

Well so was I.

Regardless, he was just going to follow me until I got into his car. I stood there, making him wait just a bit longer. Which was possibly selfish, but I wanted to punish him somehow. For hurting me. For making me feel less than.

I wanted to punish him for making me miss my old life. The one where I fit in. The one where I never felt broken. The one I was secure in.

It was also the one where I'd never felt the way Ryker made me feel. All giddy and excited. I wasn't sure I wanted to go back to the way it was before. I liked the excitement. And I liked Ryker. My dad may think he was going to change me, control me, tell me how to live my life now that I lived under his roof. Because of Dad's influence, Hunter might even stop Ryker from talking to me. But I would do all I could to keep that last part from happening. I wasn't Hunter. I didn't care about pleasing my dad. His approval was not needed. He'd done nothing to deserve that. He hadn't earned it. Not with me. He had taken Hunter when he left North Carolina and never once asked me to go too.

CHAPTER 13

RYKER

If there had been a play where Hunter could tackle me, then he'd have taken the opportunity. He'd have gotten hurt. Pretty boy was meant to throw the ball, not give a hit. But the way he glared at me during practice hadn't gone unnoticed by anyone on the team. I took it. I didn't toss back a challenge, which was completely against my nature. This was all too important. Aurora was too important. I had to prove I wasn't a dick to Hunter and completely serious about getting to know her. He was my only obstacle. I had hoped our earlier talk had eased his mind some. I could see his cracking in practice for the first time, and showing emotion meant he'd had time to think it over today, and he was still against me.

Once practice was over, he stalked off to the locker room instead of getting in my face with a threat, like I had been mentally preparing myself for. I'd worked out what to say and how to handle it. Instead I was left to follow him to the locker room. Where he continued to ignore me. I listened as the others carried on as always. The difference was that I wasn't joining in on the noise, and neither was Hunter. We were silent. I was waiting, and he was . . . Hell, I didn't know what he was doing.

"You're absolutely sure you like her enough to do this?" Nash asked me. He seemed annoyed. I didn't care. He'd annoyed me enough the past six months. He was due some in return.

"Yes," I said through gritted teeth. I'd already told him as much.

He sighed. "Then get the shit handled. Fast."

Hunter had struggled during practice today. His head had been elsewhere, and it was obvious. It confused the coach. He was the only one who didn't know what was wrong with our superstar. This wasn't my fault. He was the one who needed to let me talk. Give me a fucking chance.

Hunter looked my way then as he tossed his duffel over his shoulder. Then, before he left the room, he nodded his head toward the door as if to tell me to follow him. "Looks like it's time," I told Nash, then grabbed my bag and went to talk to Hunter.

"Do I need to come?" Nash asked. Which translated to "Are you going to hurt our quarterback?"

"It's fine. I swear," I assured him.

"It better be," he warned.

I glanced down at my phone before I stuck it in my pocket and paused when I saw a text from Aurora. Reading something from her would be what I needed to keep me levelheaded while dealing with Hunter again.

Would you come get me?

Not what I'd been expecting. Which meant something was wrong. For her to ask me that, she wasn't okay. She'd not asked Hunter. Concern grew as my imagination took over, and I almost missed Hunter standing in a neutral area between our two vehicles.

"You can't be friends with my sister. I know you say that's what you want, but it can't happen. There's a play here. You want more than that. I know how she looks. Guys always look at her," he said, his voice even and calm.

"There is no game, and yes, eventually I'd like more. I like Aurora. I've never liked a girl the way I do her. I respect her. I like talking to her—"

"She can't hear," he said, interrupting me.

I was aware he was her brother, but the way he said

that—as if it meant that what I had said didn't make sense—
pissed me off. "I don't see how that has anything to do with
it," I shot back at him.

I could see the flash of guilt in his eyes. He realized
what he had said. I hoped he had never said anything like
that to her. "I meant that there can't be much talking to her.
She only uses her voice with me. Sometimes Dad."

"She reads lips. She texts. And Tallulah can teach me
to sign."

He opened his mouth and closed it. Then stared at me as
if he wasn't sure what to say. I stood there and let him think
about it. At least he wasn't yelling or cursing at me. This
was much calmer than expected. Several guys had walked
by at a distance, going to their cars. They were all trying
not to act as if they were looking our way, but they were.

"You're willing to learn to sign? Do you have any idea
how difficult it is?"

"If it means I can communicate easier with Aurora,
then yes."

"You barely know her."

"I know I want to have a chance to get to know her
better. She's worth it."

He ran a hand through his hair and sighed with
frustration. This wasn't what he'd wanted me to say. It
was obvious he was trying to get me to back away. "I have

no problem with you, Ryker. I like you. But Aurora . . . she's . . ." He paused. "My dad will never be okay with her dating you."

The last part he said in a rush, as if saying it was the last thing he wanted to do. It was similar to his parting comment earlier today. Making it even more clear what he wanted to say but was afraid to.

"He doesn't know me," I replied. I could lie to myself and pretend I didn't know what he was trying to say. It wasn't that I was clueless. I just wanted Hunter to say it. Admit it.

He didn't, though. He stood there staring off over my left shoulder, scowling. I couldn't be sure if the scowl was for me or his dad or the fact I wasn't "picking up on it." After the seconds passed in silence, I finally decided to get to the point.

"I'm black. Say it," I told him.

Hunter closed his eyes a moment as if he wished he could be anywhere else but right here with me, having this conversation. Then he opened them and looked directly at me. "Yes."

It was one word. It didn't surprise me. This wasn't a first for me either.

"Aurora doesn't seem to give a shit about my skin color."

Hunter nodded once. "I know. Neither do I. But our dad—" He stopped again.

"Your dad doesn't want his daughter dating a black guy. How very backward of him." I couldn't keep the disgust out of my tone.

"I won't argue with you about that. I agree with you." The honesty in his voice wasn't lost on me. He meant it.

"Your dad's prejudice isn't going to stop me." And I meant that.

He shrugged. "But it may stop my sister. He isn't someone who will allow her to make her own choice."

His dad controlled him. That I'd already decided, but this only confirmed it. He wanted to please his father, and he followed the rules. I wondered then if he even had his own identity, or was he created by his father. The idea made me feel sorry for Hunter Maclay. He may have been her twin, but I decided he didn't know Aurora that well. I might have just met her, but I knew enough to know she wasn't going to let her dad's issues with skin color stop her from seeing me. Or giving me a chance at least. There was a sass in her. She didn't listen to others' opinions. She was proving that by still talking to me.

"It won't," I said with certainty.

He started to say more, then stopped.

I had given him all the time I was going to. Aurora's

text was waiting on my response. I didn't give one damn about her dad's issues with me. I was going to go get her, even if it was at her house.

"Are we done?" I asked him instead of walking away.

He nodded. "Yeah. I guess we are."

I left him then. With my phone in hand.

Where are you? I texted Aurora back.

Two seconds later she replied.

Home.

Abort Mission
CHAPTER 14

AURORA

Dad thought I was in my room. He'd gone to his office in the basement after he'd made me hug him. I'd pretended like I was fine. Ella had told him I was a teenage girl, and my being emotional was expected. She underestimated my lip-reading abilities. I was insulted by her excuse for my being upset. She hadn't been told how to live her life by my father. Not yet anyway. I knew from his body language that he was trying to act as if he was letting it go and all was well. He wasn't. This wasn't over. My dad hated to lose.

More reason to go outside and wait for Ryker. If Dad found out what I was doing, he'd be furious. I'd be grounded. Or possibly homeschooled. But then who would do that? Ella? The idea made me laugh. If Ryker got here before Hunter, this should be easy. If Hunter got here first, then it might be an issue. At least it was dark earlier now. Headlights in this neighborhood at six p.m. were normal. Lots of neighbors getting home from work.

With each set of approaching headlights, I wondered if it was Ryker. Anxious for him to get here and also nervous. My texting him and asking him to come get me was a big deal for me. I barely knew him. I had never asked a guy to come get me before that I wasn't related to. Not even Denver. The fact he had asked where I was and then said he was on his way made me feel that giddiness that seemed attached only to him.

He made me act and feel different than any guy I had ever been around. It was scary but exhilarating, too. There was nothing boring with Ryker. The fact I couldn't hear and he didn't sign was an issue, and I knew it. Our communicating wouldn't be that easy, but it was possible. I had to remind myself that he could get tired of me. I hadn't even gotten in his car yet, and I was sad thinking about it.

Guard your heart with this one, Aurora. I was telling myself that sternly when the headlights drew closer and finally this time pulled into the driveway. It was Ryker. It was a truck, but it wasn't Hunter's, which meant it had to be Ryker's. I knew Hunter could be right behind him, so I didn't pause or wait for him to get out. This wasn't a date. It was an escape. Or a rescue. Whatever, I was in a hurry.

Climbing into his truck, I smiled at him and silently said the words *thank you*.

He grinned, and I felt my own smile grow. There was no need to tell him we needed to hurry. He already knew that, because he quickly pulled out and went the opposite way from where he had come. Just like he knew I needed to get out quickly, he also knew Hunter would be coming the same way he had from the school.

The darkness kept me from seeing his lips. I couldn't talk to him while he was driving. Watching outside the window, I wondered where we were going. I had asked him to come get me. I'd not told him why, and he hadn't asked. I wasn't sure what he was planning on doing now. Surprisingly I didn't care.

His truck smelled good. Like him. I liked it. The darkness, the warmth, his scent. We could ride around for hours, and I would be okay with it. Although I doubted he would agree with me. Especially if he paid for his own gas.

The subdivision I lived in was behind us, and the road was darker and lined with woods instead of houses. I glanced at Ryker to see him relaxed as he drove with one hand on the wheel. His head turned to me for just a moment, and even though all the light we had was from the dashboard illuminating his face, it was easy to see the wink he gave me before he turned his attention back to the road.

It was simply a wink. However, like his wink yesterday, it made me tingle. I looked back out the window as my cheeks turned warm. The darkness masking my reaction. Biting my bottom lip to keep from beaming like a dork, I once again wondered where we were going.

Just as the thought came to me, he slowed and turned onto a dirt road I hadn't seen. This should worry me. It was the woods. No house around. Nothing around at all, and he was driving me down a dirt road that I would admit was very worn. It must be used often. Maybe his house was back here?

That seemed unlikely. This didn't appear to lead to any civilization. There were no lights up ahead. For the first time since I'd climbed into his vehicle I was getting nervous. I'd imagined we might go to town, or maybe his house. A dirt road that led to nowhere was not what I had bargained on, and suddenly his wink and sexy grin didn't matter. I wanted to go home. Abort mission.

A clearing . . . we were in a clearing. A large area with no trees. One old truck that didn't look as if it had been driven in a long time and some old tractor tires scattered about, a few logs, and a spot where a bonfire had been. A lot of bonfires, if I was to guess. It wasn't a new setup. This had been here. My flash of fear was now curiosity.

Ryker rolled to a stop, and then the lights came on. The outside was now even darker with the brightness inside.

"Welcome to the field. It's where all the parties are held," he said, and although I couldn't hear his voice, I could tell that he was proud of this place.

Parties? I asked without using my voice and wondering how well he could read lips.

He nodded. "Yes. Every Friday night, win or lose, during football season. Saturday nights too. Sometimes we have them for special occasions on other dates."

I wanted to explore it. Ask questions. Reluctantly I took my phone from my pocket and texted him.

Can we walk around?

He realized what I was doing, and when I glanced up, he already had his phone in his hand, reading. He nodded when his eyes met mine. Ready to see a part of his world, I reached for the door handle and opened it to climb out. It seemed too dark to see anything at first, but my eyes were already adjusting to the moonlight as I walked around the front of the car to meet Ryker. He had his phone in his hand. Ready to communicate.

Whose land is this? I sent the text and lifted my head immediately for his answer.

He read it, then met my gaze. "My dad and uncle. It was my grandfather's land. It's been used for field parties since they were in high school. Tradition."

That was not the answer I was expecting. *Wow*, I mouthed. That was a much cooler answer than I'd anticipated. This was for high school field parties. How unique.

Teenagers out here alone could get away with a lot. I glanced out at the dark woods and wondered what went on at these parties. Then my eyes saw a beer keg on the bed of the old truck. I'd never had beer from a keg, but I had seen one in more than one episode of *That '70s Show*. I recognized it even from a distance.

I took my phone and asked:

They let you drink?

Then I waited to see if he laughed at my question.

He didn't look up as quickly this time. For a second I thought he wasn't going to answer me; then finally his head lifted slowly, and his eyes locked with mine. He didn't say anything. I knew the answer without him saying it. It wasn't like I was going to call the police.

Then he nodded just once. His eyes never leaving mine. He was waiting on me to do or say something. I just wasn't sure what.

CHAPTER 15

RYKER

Disappointing a girl wasn't something I'd ever thought about. Not once had it crossed my mind. However, right now I was scared. In less than sixty seconds every mistake or bad decision I had ever made dumped on my head, and I was sure it all stood around me in neon lights. One big warning for Aurora to run from me.

She didn't run, but then those neon lights weren't actually there. As she stared at me with those incredible eyes, I wanted nothing more than to be the good guy that was worthy of her. Damn. This wasn't going to end well.

She began texting, and I waited. I hated not being able to see her eyes when she was telling me something. Learning to sign was at the top of my priority list as of tonight. I'd find something online. There had to be YouTube videos with lessons.

When she began to lift her head, I looked down at my phone as the screen lit up.

It's okay. You look like you think I'm about to call the cops. Not my plan. I was just curious.

I realized I was smiling at my phone and looked back up at her. "Good to know. But I wasn't worried about that," I told her.

She tilted her head slightly to the left; her gaze was curious, and without words I knew she was asking what I was worried about.

"I . . ." Then I paused, because I wasn't sure how to say this. There was a lot in my past I didn't want her to know. Things I couldn't go back and change. If I made her question that, either I had to tell her or someone else would. Giving her some form of the truth without being completely open was the best idea.

"I don't want to disappoint you." The brutal truth came out. It wasn't smooth at all.

She stepped toward me, and I watched her as she closed the little space between us. Then she shook her head. "You didn't." There was a whisper of her words. If she hadn't been so close, I would have missed it. I didn't know if she had even realized she'd done it. But there was sound. I'd heard her voice. Never had I thought much about someone's voice. It had been something I took for granted.

When the soft sound slammed against my chest as if I had just been given a precious, priceless gift, I had to take a moment to regroup. Get myself together. Not gape at her like an idiot.

She ducked her head, and I knew my silence had confused her. When she stepped back, my hand shot out and circled her arm gently. I liked that she had come close to me. Trusted me. I didn't want her to move away. She was looking at my hand on her arm; then she met my eyes again with her own. There was vulnerability there. My chest ached.

"You spoke." I said the words to her.

She inhaled deeply, then nodded.

"It was . . ." I didn't know how to say this. I had to say it correctly. "Thank you," I blurted. "For trusting me. For letting me hear you."

Even in the darkness I could see her face turn red. She was embarrassed, and that wasn't what I had meant to do. I wanted to hear her again. I wanted her to be secure with her voice around me. "Aurora, your voice is beautiful. Just like you are. Perfect."

She studied me then, or she studied my lips. As if she

hadn't been sure she understood me correctly. I said the same words again. Slowly, as her eyes stayed on my mouth. Her expression was so damn vulnerable I was having to fight the urge to grab her and pull her against me, to hold her. Reassure her. This was a night of firsts for me, because that sure as hell had never been an urge I'd had before.

She lifted her eyes to mine, and we stood there in the silence. The moonlight around us. There was no need for more words, but I could look at her forever. She was perfect. I hadn't been just saying that to her. I meant it.

Maybe it was the way her eyes went soft, or the warmth from her body being so close, but I didn't think. I didn't plan. I moved on instinct. The small space between us was gone, and my hands were cupping the soft skin on her cheeks as my lips covered hers. Plump and much like silk, her mouth opened slightly as she gasped softly from surprise. This was stepping over that friend line I had drawn. But I'd not believed for a moment that friendship with her was all we'd have.

She didn't move back. She didn't slap me. Her hands touched my arms so gently it was almost like a feather grazing my skin. When my tongue ran out to taste her lips, those hands grabbed on to me, no longer unsure. It was as if she was in need of support. Or possibly terrified, but I didn't stop. She wasn't pushing me off. It felt more like she was bringing me closer. Afraid I'd disappear. I understood that all too well.

If I woke up and this was a dream, then . . . fuck . . . I wasn't thinking about that right now. Nothing could ever be more real than this. But I knew it was different. Not like other times, and I wasn't going to react the way I normally would.

Aurora was giving me this. I wouldn't ruin it by pushing for more. I didn't want to think about what she had done with Denver, but I was willing to bet it wasn't much. She had the air of innocence that I normally stayed clear of. With Aurora it drew me in.

Slowly she broke the kiss, moving back just enough to inhale deeply, as if she had been holding her breath. I closed my eyes and took in the scent of her, the warmth of her body. Knowing it was about to end, I needed to memorize every detail to remember later.

Most girls would say something now. Feel the need to talk. That wasn't going to happen with Aurora. She had shared her voice with me once and so very quietly. I wanted more, but it was obvious she wasn't secure with it. I didn't want to push her.

I realized the inability to use words right now was a gift instead of a difficulty. Holding her with nothing but the night around us gave me a chance to use my hand to caress her face, feel the way she relaxed into me and trusted me. All things I had never experienced before. Because it hadn't happened or because I never gave this a chance.

My past wasn't going to ruin this moment. I closed that part off when those thoughts began to resurface. Reminding me how I wasn't worthy of someone like Aurora. Yet here she was with me. She'd called me when she needed to escape her house. I still didn't know why she'd wanted to leave, but it had been me she turned to.

Her hand touched my chest, and then she pushed back away from me. Her head tilted up to meet my eyes. I saw the light in them. The happiness. She didn't regret this. She wasn't moving away from me because she was ending it.

"Okay, I'll use my voice." She said the words louder this time, but they were still soft. The emotions in my chest weren't describable, nor the way I had been completely humbled. Possibly for the first time in my life.

Yeah, Life Is Different Now

CHAPTER 16

AURORA

The happy glow that had followed me inside the house and up to my bedroom was wiped out the moment my eyes met Hunter's. He was standing at the window with his arms crossed over his chest, staring at me.

"Dad could have been in the living room. Did you think of that?" he signed.

Actually I had, but only briefly. I shrugged. I didn't want to be reminded of Dad or the argument we'd had earlier.

"I like Ryker. But Dad isn't going to like this," he continued.

I wasn't worried about Dad or his likes. Not like

Hunter was. I wouldn't say that, though. I often felt sorry
for my brother. He had never been able to make is own
choices. He never fought back. It was as if he had gotten
the hearing, but I'd been given all the backbone.

"I don't care who likes this," I said, hoping that hadn't
been too loud. Just because I felt bad for Hunter and
wished he'd step out and do what he wanted to do didn't
mean I was happy about the fact he was in here bursting
my bubble.

"Did you break up with Denver?" He threw that at me,
and I hadn't been expecting it.

Again I shrugged. I wasn't sure we were even a thing
that had to be broken up. He'd not been acting like it. "I
think that's over, but I will make sure tomorrow."

Hunter sighed and shook his head. "This is going to
be bad. You are in school two days. Two days, Aurora,
and you decide you like Ryker Lee. Why so soon and why
him?"

If he liked Ryker, then why was he being so dramatic
about this? I had never been one to try and please our dad.
He knew that, or had he forgotten how things had been
before he moved away? Why act like Dad could force me
into anything now? Instead of asking him all that, I told
him, "I've never felt like this about anyone before." There,
he could chew on that. Ryker made my world light up. It

didn't matter it had only been two days. Was that supposed to take time? I didn't think so, because I'd had years with Denver, and not once had he made me feel like Ryker did from the moment I saw him.

"You've never dated other guys to give them a chance. It's always been Denver. You have no idea. You just met Ryker. He's new. It's exciting. He has sex with different girls every night. Sometimes two different girls in a weekend. Friday night he had sex with Nova. I've seen them in the halls together this week."

The girl he'd been arguing with today. He'd had sex with her Friday? Was that what they were fighting about? Or talking about? Ryker didn't seem like a guy who would do that, but then I was just getting to know him.

The memory of Ryker's kiss, the way he looked at me, held me . . . could the same guy have casual sex with girls? It didn't fit. He was sweet. Gentle. I shook my head, refusing to believe the rumors. Unless Hunter was there watching them, which I knew he hadn't been, it was just talk. Words.

"Where did y'all go tonight?" he asked then.

"The field," I told him, knowing he knew about the field.

Hunter frowned. "Did he try anything?"

That was it. This was over. Hunter was actually asking me if I'd done things with Ryker. Was he serious right now? Ryker's reputation was obviously much worse than I'd realized if Hunter would think that. I needed to evaluate things, but not with my brother's help. I pointed to my door and said, "Not your business. Leave."

Hunter started to say something, so I looked away. Silencing him. He hated it when I did that. When we were kids, I called it my superpower. It still was.

Hunter walked to stand in front of me. I closed my eyes. I wasn't listening anymore. I was also acting like I was five years old, but that didn't matter. My mind was currently battling with this news about Ryker and if it was true.

I slowly opened my eyes after standing there for a few moments to find Hunter waiting on me to do just that.

"I know this has been hard on you," Hunter said this time with his words and signing. "The move and everything changing. I want you to be happy. I just know you won't be if Dad finds out. He won't be okay with it. He'll be furious. Is Ryker worth that? I can only lie for you so long. At some point he will catch you, or hear about it; this town isn't big."

I understood everything he was saying. But again, Hunter was asking because he always cowered to our father's wishes. Or *demands* would be a better term. I didn't. I wasn't starting now. Not with the cochlear implant and not with Ryker. The idea that my dad cared about skin color bothered me more than the fact that he wanted me to become what he thought I should be. His controlling issues were one thing; his being racist was more than disappointing—it was embarrassing.

"My life. My choices," I told Hunter firmly. I bit my tongue to keep from saying that I wished he'd find his own life too and stop living Dad's version of it. He'd get defensive. It would do no good.

Hunter finally gave me a nod. "Okay. I'll do what I can to help," he said, but his eyes looked worried. I read that without knowing how his voice sounded. "Just know it's not rumors. Last week he was bragging about screwing a college girl. His words. His bragging. I was there. I heard him say it. He likes you, and I hope he respects you. But I also know how he is. You need to know who you're trusting."

I stood there and said nothing. Hunter left then, closing my door behind him. Ryker talking about having sex made me feel insecure, oddly enough. A college girl? He was charming and attractive enough to get college girls. But he'd bragged about it. He was comfortable with college girls and sex. I wasn't what he was used to. I had a more sheltered life than most girls my age. I knew it. It was something I needed to think about. I wasn't the kind of girl to go have sex in the woods at a field party, which was what

I kind of wondered was happening when I had seen the place. Rubbing my temples, I groaned and thought about my brother being so protective.

My mom had never been this interested in my life. She had let me make my own decisions. Never questioning me. But then my mother had always been very focused on her own life. I wasn't sure which was worse: her not caring or Hunter, and Dad for that matter, caring too much.

Leaving my home and all I knew had been hard, though meeting Ryker had made it worth it. He made me feel as if he'd flipped on a switch and my world was brighter. I smiled more. Felt giddy when, before, I hadn't even understood what being giddy meant. I got it now.

Ryker made me excited for the change my life had taken. The vibration of my phone caught my attention, and I was already grinning before looking at it. Expecting to see Ryker's name on the screen. Even with all this new knowledge I had been given about him, I wanted to talk to him.

My smile fell when I saw Denver's name instead. He was a reminder that I had to close that part of my life. I'd never had to do something like this before, and I wasn't sure how to do it. Even if Ryker couldn't be more to me than a friend. He needed to know I wasn't like the other girls. I wasn't casual about sex. The kiss he'd given me was earth shattering for me. Which made my ignorance with that kind of thing a larger barrier to getting closer to Ryker.

How are things? Haven't heard from you. Hope that means you are settling in okay.

It would have been easier if he didn't seem to truly care. This was caring. This was Denver. Polite, kind, good sense of humor. All those things were great, but it was also the exact same way he treated everyone. There was nothing special with how he treated me. But he wasn't sleeping with a lot of girls either. He was safe. I never had those concerns with Denver.

Things are good. I like it here. I like the school, the people.

It was here I should tell him about Ryker. But I paused. *Do I just say it? Get it over with?* I waited for Denver's response, wishing he would do it. End it. Give us the closure we needed. I wouldn't feel guilty or have any regrets if it was Denver who said this was impossible. I had known when I left that the distance would be an issue. But he hadn't ended it then. Never even mentioned ending it.

That's awesome. I was afraid your silence meant you hated it. I've already asked my mom if I could come visit you. Try and cheer you up.

My stomach felt a little sick. He had been thinking of coming here? I didn't expect that. He hadn't been texting me or seeming as if he missed me at all. Why would he want to come here? Did he miss me? Was I so wrapped up in Ryker that I forgot my feelings for Denver?

No. Ryker just made me face how I felt about Denver. How I'd always felt about him. He was my friend. Possibly my best friend. We had become comfortable together. Friends to dating, when the time came. There had never been a real spark, and Ryker had been the one to show me that, even if he hadn't meant to.

That's nice of you.

I could think of nothing else to say, and I knew reading it that it sounded lame. Not at all the response he would be expecting. My finger hovered over send as I tried to think of anything else to add. I was so bad at this. Hunter would know what I should say, but I wasn't asking him. Not when he was pro Denver. Closing my eyes tightly, I clicked send and kept my eyes closed, wondering if he'd get the hint. Hating how this felt.

Three minutes ticked by with no response. I chewed on my bottom lip nervously. He was thinking that over. He knew me well. My short response said so much. Then the phone vibrated in my hand, and my eyes slowly opened with dread.

I'm home. Did you get in trouble for the escape?

Ryker. The jumble of emotions I'd been dealing with over Denver's text vanished instantly, and I was grinning again. Ryker didn't have to do much to make me smile. I touched my lips, thinking about how his had felt against mine. It had been magical. My cheeks flushed. It was hard to remember or believe what my brother had told me about him. I started to reply to him when another text lit the screen.

Are we okay? The distance is weird.

Denver. He was getting to the point. Dealing with it head-on. Very Denver. I wanted to talk to Ryker and feel all the excitement that came with him. But this had to be done. Handled. It was only fair. The right thing to do. Even if this was a mistake, and I found out that I'd been wrong about Ryker, I knew I was wasting Denver's time. Holding on to the past. Something he didn't even realize wasn't special. I'd been his first and only girlfriend. I typed out the words he needed to hear. The ones that would set him free.

I don't see how we can remain exclusive while we are this far apart. Life is different now.

I should say more. I just didn't know what. And was exclusive a silly way of explaining what we were? This was my first breakup, but it would be Denver's, too. Neither of us knew what to do, say, or expect. I felt a pang of sadness. Not because I was ending this or because I loved Denver. He was just another part of my past I was letting go.

After sending it, I went to Ryker's text and replied.

No one knew I was gone but Hunter. He was fine with it. Thank you for coming to my rescue.

I didn't think telling Ryker about Hunter's lecture was helpful. I had questions about his sex life. I had questions about the girl in the hallway today. Was this only exciting for me? Did Ryker see me as he did every other girl? I pushed all those questions aside. Ryker was texting me, and I didn't want to spoil my mood.

Yeah, life is different now.

That was the last text I got from Denver that night, but I didn't realize it until the next day. I'd gotten engrossed in talking to Ryker.

CHAPTER 17

RYKER

Nova pulled up right beside me when I got to school the next morning. I knew it was on purpose, and I prepared myself for whatever this was about. She'd texted me several times last night, and I hadn't replied. Most girls would get pissy, ignore me, or just glare at me. Nova, however, wasn't going away that easily. Even after she'd told me yesterday it was over and she was done with me, she'd sent me three snaps I had left unopened just last night. My guess was she wasn't wearing much or anything in them.

Texting with Aurora had kept me up until after two, when she'd fallen asleep. I wasn't big into Snapchat, but I was going to see if Aurora had it on her phone. I'd like to see her face when talking to her on the phone. She didn't come across as a selfie kind of girl, though.

Getting out of my truck, I grabbed my backpack and sighed, trying to prepare myself for the drama. I did a quick glance for Hunter's truck and didn't see it. Which meant Aurora wasn't here yet.

"Do you not want to see my snaps, or were you asleep last night?" Nova asked as she sauntered up to me and smirked. She had more confidence than any female I knew. That was good. Because she wouldn't get all weepy when I was blunt with her. Again.

"I thought you were done with me. You should be. I'm interested in someone else." That was as honest as I could get.

She rolled her eyes. "You fall in and out of interest with girls more than I change my panties. When I'm even wearing panties." She was flirting. Trying to get me to think about her in panties. It wasn't working. I didn't care. If I wanted to see her in panties or out of them, I would have opened her snaps.

"This is different," I said, wishing she'd leave me alone.

Nova laughed. "Yes, she's different all right. You're not going to last long. She's too sweet and a goody-goody. It's all over her face."

That annoyed me. Aurora was sweet and good, but

saying it like those were bad traits only made it clear Nova was neither. She wasn't a mean person. She just wasn't Aurora. It was also apparent that people were noticing my interest in Aurora. I liked that. I wanted to make sure no one else decided to move in on her. I had to win her over first.

"We will be just fine," I said, not trying to get her to stay around and continue to talk to me. I kept my eyes on the parking lot for Hunter's vehicle.

"Don't think I'll be waiting on you to figure out this won't work with her. I like you, but you're not that damn special." Nova was angry and trying not to show it. She had liked me. She did like me. I knew that. She wouldn't be pushing this so hard if she wasn't upset that I didn't return the feelings.

"I don't expect that," I said just as I saw Hunter's truck. "I gotta go," I added, and turned from her to walk toward where Hunter was parking.

"You will regret this!" she called out. I'd heard that from her already. I also knew I wasn't going to regret it. She wasn't stable. I'd sensed that this weekend and stopped from going too far with her. Saying as much, though, was cruel. I wasn't that guy now. Or I didn't want to be that guy. I walked toward Aurora instead.

Aurora stepped down out of the truck, and I had to

admit that the fact that her eyes were already on me felt good. Too good. Seeing her this morning, remembering our kiss, was like she had brought me back to life. It was terrifying to admit, but it was also amazing.

"Good morning, beautiful." I said the words, not caring who heard me. She returned my smile, and I watched her tuck a strand of hair behind her ear nervously.

"Good morning," she said almost too softly, but I heard her. I loved the sound of it, no matter how soft the whisper. I wondered if she knew she was whispering or if that was something she could even gauge. There was so much I didn't know about her life that I wanted to know and understand.

"She used her voice," Hunter said, and the amazement in his tone wasn't missed by me.

I didn't want to look his way to speak, but I knew if I replied to him while looking at her she'd be confused. She hadn't heard him. He could just take that piece of information and deal with it however he wanted.

"Did you sleep good?" I asked her, knowing she hadn't gotten that many hours of sleep, and neither had I. Saying good night and ending our conversation last night wasn't something I had been willing to do. Which is why we texted until she fell asleep.

She nodded and blushed. Her eyes cut toward Hunter,

who was watching us. I wanted her not to care that he was there or what he was thinking. But he was her brother, and I knew she didn't like him hearing us.

I reached down and took her hand in mine, then said, "Let's go," so she could read my lips clearly.

We made our way to the entrance, and our joined hands were drawing attention. I hoped she didn't notice or that if she did, she didn't care. I wanted them all to know. I was making this real clear. Yesterday I'd been interested in her, but with one kiss it had all changed. I was in completely.

She'd broken up with Denver officially last night. We'd talked about it, and I'd let out a loud cheer in my room when I'd read the text about it. I had thought winning her over would take more time. But her honesty was admirable. She said she couldn't keep talking to me and not break things off with Denver.

"When did she start using her voice with you?" Hunter asked. I hadn't realized he was walking so closely behind us.

"Last night," I said, not looking at him but straight ahead.

"She didn't tell me that." He seemed truly confused. "She only uses her voice with me and Dad. Not even Ella, our stepmom."

That was information she might not want me to know, but I was glad he'd told me. It was already special to me, but now it was precious. Never had I thought about long term in anything. I lived in the moment. Then I moved on to the new.

With Aurora that was changing. Everything was changing. I glanced down at her beside me; last night might have been my last first kiss. That should have scared the hell out of me. Instead I was scared that this was impossible. That her dad would make sure there was no future. My hand tightened on hers, and she lifted her gaze to meet mine. Then she smiled, and it eased my fear.

My past, as in last week, was still there waiting for her to find out. When she heard the truth about me, I would have to make a lot of promises and work to prove to her this was different for me. I didn't want to be the guy I was a week ago. I didn't miss him.

She would know soon enough. I had to get over that hurdle too. Not just her dad not liking the fact I was black.

CHAPTER 18

AURORA

I was doing my best not to think about seeing Ryker with that girl again when we got to school this morning. Hunter had made a point to tell me, "That's the one he slept with Friday night," before I could get out of the truck.

I shrugged it off. Not thinking about it. Either Hunter was very wrong about Ryker, or I was. I doubted Hunter had ever talked to him as much as I had already. He didn't know Ryker.

During lunch, the girl had watched us. I'd looked over and caught her glaring our way. But only that once. I didn't want her to think I cared. She was frightening. Should I ask Ryker about her? Or was that too soon? Not my business? I wish I had someone to ask about these things.

I could ask Tallulah, but then she seemed to think the same of Ryker as Hunter did. I needed an unbiased opinion. My mother possibly? Ryker had held my hand every chance he got today. He'd shown up to walk me to classes, and it had just made Hunter grumpy. He was still not happy about this. But he was at least keeping quiet.

Ella picked me up after school with her ever-present smile. She didn't say much, because conversing with me made her nervous. As if she was going to offend me or something. I wasn't sure what her issue was. The good thing about it was that there was no pointless conversation with Ella to deal with. I was alone with my thoughts on the ride home and in my room while I did my homework, then decided to read.

This was similar to how life had been back in North Carolina. It was comfortable, but now my thoughts were always drifting toward Ryker and what he was doing. Where he was . . . and sometimes who he was with. Even though I knew he was at football practice, just like Hunter, my imagination kept picturing the girl, Nova, waiting on him when it was over. That made me feel bad. I wasn't sure I liked the constant thinking about it or him.

When my phone vibrated at six, I couldn't deny the

thrill of excitement as I reached into my pocket to get it. Seeing Ryker's name made me smile big, and I didn't know what I was going to do with this mix of emotions. I knew practice was over at six. He had to have texted me as soon as it ended. Which meant there was no girl waiting on him.

Can you leave?

It was a simple text. No explanation. But then yesterday I'd asked him to come get me with no explanation.

Yes.

I hit send, thinking leaving might be harder than yesterday. I wasn't sure where Dad was, and Hunter would be here any minute. This wasn't how I wanted to do things with Ryker. If my father would be okay with him just coming to the door, talking a little, and then taking me out, that would be simple. Normal.

Do I pick you up outside?

I hated saying yes. It made me feel like I was hiding him. Hunter was our dad's project after all. Ryker's skin color was a ridiculous reason to tell me I wasn't allowed to see him. His reputation may be an issue, but Dad could talk to him. Would Dad do that? Act like a normal parent and listen to Ryker? Let Ryker promise to respect me, et cetera? I wasn't Dad's project child. He had never put his hand in my decisions. He'd only spoken to Denver once. None of this made me feel comfortable telling Ryker to come to the door. I didn't trust my father. He had lost his last attempt to control me. I wasn't sure he'd be ready to have me ignore his idea on how I should live my life so soon. I needed some time to deal with him first.

Yes. But just this time. I'm going to change that.

I sent it but wondered how I was going to change that. Shoving that fear aside, I glanced down at my clothes. I was still in what I had worn to school today. Yesterday I hadn't thought about what I was going to wear when me picked me up. Now it mattered. I was thinking about it. Admitting to myself it was because I couldn't get the image of Nova out of my mind or the faceless college girl he'd been with recently. It made me feel shallow. Without even meaning to, I had started trying to compete with these girls. Truth was, I couldn't compete with Nova or the college girl. Not if it came down to sex. I wasn't ready for that. Not with Denver, who I had dated for years, and definitely not with a guy I had just met. I knew nothing about sex. Except for what I'd read in books.

Ryker was going to have to like me for me. Not because of what I wore or what I was willing to do with my body. Saying that to myself was easy. Remembering it was hard. Because as I glanced in the mirror, I was again thinking I should change. Maybe into some leggings and the off-the-shoulder sweater I had gotten from Mom right before I moved. I hadn't worn it yet. I was saving it for something special. This wasn't a date. My guess was we were headed back to the field.

Headlights from Hunter's truck flashed in the windows, and I sighed. It wasn't like Ryker was a secret from him, but telling Hunter I was leaving with Ryker was going to lead to another conversation I didn't want to have.

I'll be there in 15.

Ryker's text lit up the screen, and I looked from his words to the new sweater in my closet. Debating hard and forgetting about my brother. Dropping my phone to the bed, I rushed to grab the sweater and change into it before I could decide against this. It was green and matched my eyes. I liked wearing green because of this. Then I chose a pair of black leggings. Quickly I changed out of the jeans and pale blue long-sleeved pullover I'd worn today.

Running a brush through my hair, I studied myself in the mirror and decided to add a little lip gloss. Once I was done with that, I grabbed my black ankle boots and slipped them on. The more I did to myself the more nervous I got. Being attractive to Ryker had suddenly become very important.

My door opened slightly and closed three times. Then he waited. This was how Hunter came to my door. It was his way of asking if he could come in. I walked over and opened the door. My brother took in my appearance, then sighed. He knew where I was going. There was no reason to even ask me.

"You're going somewhere with Ryker?" He said the words, but I had no doubt he did so silently, and signed at the same time. He wouldn't want Dad or Ella hearing him. Although Ella probably had no interest in who Ryker was. She didn't get involved in my life, and from what I could see, she wasn't at all involved in Hunter's. But then neither had my mother been involved with Hunter. Dad hadn't allowed that.

I nodded.

"Dad know?"

He knew Dad didn't know. If I had told Dad, we would be in the living room right now in a fierce battle, no doubt. Or at least that was what I imagined was going to happen. Hunter was sure Dad wouldn't be okay with me dating a black boy. He knew him better than anyone. I still had my doubts, because although Dad liked to make decisions for everyone, I'd never witnessed him being racist. Dad was typically charismatic with others. My mother used to explain him that way to others. He just wasn't that way behind closed doors.

I raised both eyebrows, as if his question was ridiculous, then shook my head. I had taken his word on our dad not accepting Ryker.

Hunter glanced back at the stairs, then signed, "He's in his office."

"Good," I replied, using my voice.

Hunter gave a short nod. "I'll cover for you if I need to. But be careful."

I thought that sounded a bit silly. The only person I feared currently was our dad, and that was because I wasn't like Hunter and never would be. When he realized that, I wasn't sure how he would react. He had let the cochlear implant thing go a little too easily. I felt like it was sitting there waiting to be tossed out again. Or forced upon me when I least expected it.

"Ryker isn't going to hurt me," I replied, shoving those fears aside. I didn't want to think about it now. Not when I had a date with Ryker. I wanted to enjoy the happy.

Hunter lifted a shoulder. "Just guard your emotions."

He was being a brother. I understood that. I was also running out of time. Ryker would be here soon. "I need to go," I told him, but I said so with a smile.

He stepped back and let me go.

I Could Be Her Biggest Mistake
CHAPTER 19

RYKER

My headlights were off, but I knew she saw me parked by the road when she stepped out of the house. Aurora's pale skin in the moonlight caught my attention, and I saw her left shoulder was bare. It was modest compared to what most of the girls I knew wore, but seeing her shoulder uncovered still made my hands clench the steering wheel a little tighter. She reminded me of an angel . . . and I was closer to the devil. I could be her biggest mistake. It was up to me to make sure I wasn't. I swallowed and got out of the truck to walk around and open her door.

I might have to hide in the dark to pick her up, but I

didn't like her climbing in my truck without me opening her door and helping her up. My momma wouldn't like it either. But then she wouldn't like how we were doing this. She'd be upset that I had to hide.

Aurora smiled up at me when she got to the door I was opening.

"Thank you." She used her voice again.

I couldn't say you're welcome or you're beautiful or anything because it was too dark for her to see my lips. I took her small hand in mine, and she stepped up into the truck, which I'd had jacked up a little higher than necessary. I wanted to take her by the waist and lift her, but I also didn't want to startle her. She'd gotten in by herself last night in the rush she had been in, so I knew she could get in without my hands on her body.

Closing the door behind her, I went back to the driver's seat.

I was going to have to stop staying up late texting with her and start studying sign language. Times like this I could use it. She was just hard to say good night to. I never wanted the conversation to end.

I pulled onto the road and turned toward Nash's house. I didn't want to take her to the field again. It felt too much like I was hiding her in the dark. Nash said he was going to be at Tallulah's until late. His parents were on a cruise.

Tallulah's mom wanted them at her house since his parents weren't home.

He had his own guy cave over the garage at his house. It had a large flat screen and kitchen, and just recently he'd added a pool table, since he'd rejoined the rest of the living and was not sulking in silence anymore. He had the team over regularly now, and the pool table had been an addition his mom thought we could use. All one guy needs.

I had used his place more than once in the past for sex with whoever I was with, but tonight that wasn't my plan. I had ordered a pizza, wings, and cheese bread that should be delivered in fifteen more minutes. This was more like a date than the field was.

It would also make it easier for us to communicate. That was my main goal. Seeing her face. Watching her smile. Then of course, I wanted to kiss again. She wasn't someone else's tonight. She no longer had a boyfriend. No one standing there keeping her from me. That made this more real.

I opened the garage with the remote I had gotten from Nash, wanting to be sure my truck wasn't seen, so no one would decide to stop by and say hi. Or my dad to stop by and see what I was doing. He'd see Aurora and assume the worst. My parents weren't as strict about my being alone with girls, but Nash's dad was tighter on the reins with that. His parents wouldn't be okay with me having a girl over alone.

I turned to look at her once the garage door closed behind us and I cut off the engine.

"Is this your house?" she asked me, looking a bit surprised but pleased.

I shook my head no. "Nash's house," I replied.

Her eyes widened, and she looked around the garage we had parked inside. I knew her mind was working hard to figure out why there was no one here. I opened my door, and I was almost to the other side when her door opened. I moved quickly to take her hand and help her as she stepped down. She studied my face as if the answer to her question was written there.

"Nash has his own place up there," I said, pointing to the ceiling, then the stairs behind us. "Come on."

I kept her dainty hand in my much larger one, then squeezed softly to reassure her before leading her to the stairs. I stepped back and motioned for her to go first. She did, and I followed behind, trying not to look at her butt; however, in those leggings it wasn't easy. I finally just gave in and enjoyed the view until she reached the top step.

When I joined her, I moved in beside her, then opened the door to the apartment. With a wave of my hand I motioned for her to go inside. She looked around, then went through the door as I turned on the lights. The large leather sofa and elaborate setup for a teenager was every guy's dream. In the beginning this had just been a den for the teenagers when they came over. To get us out of the house. Nash had a bedroom he still used inside the house.

After his injury, though, he'd gotten in a bad depression, and he stayed out here more and more. When he got serious with Tallulah, the sleeping out here ended. Which I thought was a little ridiculous. We were both eighteen now. We'd both be moving in the fall. Going away to college. Nash's parents needed to decide it was time to trust him to make his own decisions. If he and Tallulah were going to have sex, not letting him sleep out here wasn't going to stop that. Parents could be naive sometimes. I didn't know if they'd had sex or not. Nash didn't talk about that, but I did know I'd caught them in the middle of something where Tallulah had been without a shirt or bra once. I hadn't looked, but I let him know his dad was right behind me and they needed to get dressed fast.

Aurora finished taking the place in before turning to look at me. "This is nice," she said softly.

I nodded. "He has a great setup. I ordered pizza, wings, and cheese bread. Have you eaten?"

She smiled then and shook her head no.

"Good. It's a date, an official one."

That got a bigger smile from her. Something about making her smile made me feel like a king. If I let myself, I'd stand here and keep saying things to make her smile. I was way too deep with how I felt about her, but I didn't want her to know that yet. We had a lot to work through first. Instead of embarrassing myself with my stupid jokes and attempts at getting her to laugh, I walked over to the pool table and picked up a stick. "You play?" I figured this was more likely than the video games Nash also had connected to the TV.

She smirked then. The kind of smirk that said I had asked a dumb question. The confident nod of her head surprised me. I watched with appreciation the way she walked toward me and picked up her own stick. I'd thought this would give us something to do. I would get to teach her, possibly, but that didn't appear to be the case. I wasn't going to get a chance to stand close behind her. I wasn't sure if I was impressed or disappointed.

"Rack them." That was the loudest she'd used her voice with me. I grinned, not just because she seemed so sure of her pool-playing abilities, but also because she was getting braver with me. Trusting me with her voice.

I wanted to grab her, pull her against me, and kiss that sexy smirk off her face. It was hard not to. Keeping my hands off her was a constant struggle, it seemed. But this

was a date. Our first one. Kissing her the entire time was
not how I wanted her to remember it. I wanted her to have
fun. I wanted to laugh with her. I didn't want her to think
I'd brought her up here to get in her pants. Which was normally why I brought girls up here. Okay, it was the only
reason I had brought girls up here in the past.

This being-a-gentleman thing was foreign to me, but I
thought I was doing a pretty damn good job of it so far. I
did as she had instructed and got us racked when the door-
bell outside the garage door went off. My head jerked up to
look at the door, confused for a second, and then I realized
it was the pizza. I'd forgotten about our food.

"Food is here. I'll be right back," I told her so she'd
understand where I was going suddenly.

I ran down the stairs, wanting to hurry and get this over
with before someone saw the delivery car outside. When
I opened the back door, Rifle was standing there with the
food. I hadn't known he was working at the Pizza Slab.
This was the first time he'd delivered my food.

"I was expecting Nash," Rifle said with a smile, handing me the order as he pulled it out of the heated packaging.

"I'm borrowing the place tonight," I told him.
"Thanks," I added, then handed him a tip.

"Thank you," he said with a pleased grin at the cash in
his hand. I started to step back and close the door when he

asked, "Hey, I saw you with Aurora Maclay today a few times. Are you seeing her?"

I paused. Rifle was a junior like Aurora and a good friend of Hunter's. He was also on the team, but we weren't close. "Why?" I asked him, unsure how to handle this question. If it was up to me, I'd say yes. But I didn't know what Aurora wanted me to say.

He started to reply when his eyes lifted to look at the top of the stairs behind me. The surprise in his expression had me turning my head to look back. Aurora was standing there. She obviously had no idea what we were saying or the fact that Rifle had seen her might be an issue. I expected Hunter to show up within the hour.

"Not your business, bro," I warned him.

He jerked his gaze back to me and gave a sharp nod of understanding.

"If her brother shows up here, I'll know why." I made sure he understood that the threat in my voice was real.

His eyes widened, and he nodded again. "Thanks for the tip," he said quickly, and all but ran back to his car to get away from me.

I closed the door and locked it before heading back up the stairs to the waiting Aurora.

"Where is the bathroom?" she asked me once we were back inside the apartment.

I pointed to the door behind her and she smiled shyly, then went to use it.

I had to decide if I should tell her and let her be nervous and worried that Hunter could possibly show up. I wasn't sure if Rifle would take my threat seriously or not. Ruining our evening over a possibility that Hunter might show up would suck.

CHAPTER 20

AURORA

That had been Hunter's friend, Rifle. I remembered meeting him. Thinking how weird that name was. I stood looking in the mirror while fighting the urge to bite my nails. If he told Hunter I was here, it was very possible Hunter would show up and cause a scene. If he knew about this private den of Nash's, he'd assume the worst. Hunter said he was okay with me seeing Ryker and would cover for me if he could, but I doubted that he'd be okay with my being here alone with him. I'd seen the surprise in Rifle's face when he recognized me.

When we had come here instead of somewhere in town, I realized Ryker was trying to make this a real date, but also respecting the fact I was sneaking around to see him. He should be insulted by the fact he even had to see me secretly. I was insulted for him. I didn't like hiding or running outside in the dark to get in his truck. I shouldn't have to do that. After tonight I was telling my dad about this. He'd have to accept my dating Ryker and deal with it. That all sounded a lot easier than it would actually be.

I took a deep breath and ran my hand through my hair to smooth it, then smiled at my bare, freckled shoulder. I liked this look. I had seen Ryker looking at my skin too. He liked it. Feeling better and ready to face my brother if that was what happened, I stepped back out of the bathroom and found Ryker opening the boxes of food up on the bar.

His back was to me, and I let myself admire the way he looked in jeans from behind. His wide shoulders stretched the fabric of the pale blue cotton shirt he was wearing. He was tall, and so big it should make him intimidating, but his smile made you forget his size. My brother was tall, but he was more lean. He certainly didn't have the muscles bulging in his arms the way Ryker did. The sleeves were tight on his biceps much like his shoulders.

He turned then, and I knew my cheeks heated at being caught checking him out. The cocky grin on his face as he realized I had been looking at him made me want to laugh.

Ryker Lee had no self-esteem issues. That was for sure. He oozed confidence. It was attractive on him. He made it charming somehow instead of obnoxious, like so many guys appeared.

"Hungry?" he asked.

I nodded and walked toward him and the food he'd set out. There were two different pizzas. One for meat lovers and one without meat at all. He was good at this. Thinking about little things like that. Although I loved meat. I'd be eating the meat lovers'. Bacon was my favorite, and I could see it on the pizza.

I glanced up at him, and I caught a frown. I hadn't expected that. "What's wrong?" I asked right away.

"The guy who delivered this is a friend of your brother's."

Ah. He had thought about that too.

I nodded. "I know. Rifle—I've met him," I said.

The small wrinkle on his forehead didn't go away. "Should we expect Hunter to show up?"

I thought about it a minute. I'd worried about the same thing. Ryker didn't want tonight to be ruined either. He'd tried to make dating easy for me, and he shouldn't have to worry about that. I reached for my phone, which I'd slid into the side pocket of my leggings.

"I'm going to make sure he doesn't," I assured him.

Ryker's frown eased some. "Can you do that?"

I nodded again, not feeling as confident as I was trying to be. It was possible Hunter would flip out.

I am at Nash's house with Ryker. He ordered pizza and we are playing pool. He knows dad won't be okay with me dating him so he chose this for privacy. Nothing else is going on. Rifle delivered the pizza. He saw me here. Don't show up and ruin this night for me.

I reread it, then hit send. Then I looked back up at Ryker. "I texted him."

Ryker raised an eyebrow. "You know he doesn't trust me."

I grinned then. "I know. But he trusts me."

Ryker chuckled. I wished I could hear that. Know what it sounded like. Without thinking, I reached out and placed my hand on his chest to feel it. The rumble in his voice. The vibration. He stopped, though, the moment my hand touched him.

I lifted my eyes from his chest I had been observing and saw he was frozen. I'd confused him. He wasn't moving, and I wanted him to laugh again. I needed to know how it felt. That's all I could have. "I wanted to feel your laugh," I explained, not sure he'd get that. It sounded odd to those who didn't understand the deaf world.

My phone vibrated, and I dropped my hand from his chest and opened the text from my brother.

Ryker promised me he'd not try anything with you. I am going to trust him. But know this, I don't care about his size or that he is a crucial part of the team. I will make him regret it if he does anything wrong. Anything that disrespects you.

I wanted to be angry at Hunter's response. As if I needed a protector. But I knew it was all because he loved me. He wasn't trying to control me. He was worried about me. But he was trying to let me have a life here too.

I glanced up at Ryker, who was very still. I wanted to laugh this time. There were no worries that Ryker was going to do anything that Hunter would disapprove of. At this point I was pretty sure I would need to work just to get kissed. He was more nervous than I was.

You don't need to worry about Ryker. He's being so good I doubt I get kissed.

I thought about not sending that but decided it would keep my brother away from here tonight. So I sent it. I lifted my gaze back to Ryker, who was studying my face for answers.

"He said he is going to trust you."

Ryker let out a sigh of relief, and again I wished I could hear that. I wanted to hear him. This was new for me. I'd never craved the sound of someone's voice before. I didn't know what that was like, so it hadn't been something I'd thought too much about. The cochlear could give me things like that. Then it could go wrong, too. Not work at all.

"Good," Ryker said.

I thought about eating and returning to our game of pool but decided to be brave. Tell him what I was thinking. I'd trusted him with my voice, and although I had no idea what it sounded like, I knew it wasn't perfect. I knew it was different. That was something I'd learned in the deaf school I'd attended. They'd encouraged us to use it but told us it wouldn't always be clear to the hearing, since we may not be pronouncing correctly.

"I wanted to feel your laugh. I can't hear it. I wish I could. I've never wished that before. But I do with you."

His expression changed. His eyes held a softness inside their dark pools. His full lips parted slightly. I liked reading his lips, because it gave me a reason to study them. "That's why you touched my chest?"

I nodded but kept my eyes on his mouth.

He gave a soft smile. "I'd laugh again if I could, but right now laughing isn't what I want to do."

"Oh," I said, glancing up to meet his eyes and see if something was wrong.

He took a very slow step toward me. His eyes holding mine with that same softness that said so much in the silence. I saw his arm move to my left just as his hand touched my waist. My eyes dropped to see his hand on me. I wanted to save that in my memory to think of later. I loved the color of his skin. It reminded me of a warm, deep, ebony. It was beautiful. Just like I was sure his laugh would be. His hand squeezed my waist with very little pressure, and it gave me a thrill. I wanted to memorize that, too.

His finger slid under my chin and lifted my head back up to meet his gaze. My eyes went to his lips instead, in case he was going to say something. His hand kept the hold on my waist, and it didn't make me nervous. That surprised me. His hand was big, like the rest of him. It should have scared me a little at least, but it didn't. I wanted it there.

His lips didn't move. He said no words. Instead he moved even closer and lowered his broad shoulders and head to me as I stood on my tiptoes, knowing what was to come this time. Wanting it more than I wanted air. When his full lips met mine, I felt the sound I made. I hadn't meant to, and in the moment I couldn't worry what it had been or if it was loud.

Whatever the sound came out to be, it made his hand squeeze me again, and I felt a vibration in his chest as I placed my right hand on it for support. Sliding it to the exact spot where I could feel any sound he might make, I opened my mouth just as his lips parted over mine. The mint from his gum was the first taste as he began to make my world spin from the pleasure. Kissing him this time was more powerful than before. He made me feel weak in the knees just as the electricity of this touch tingled throughout me. It was a confusing reaction, and I didn't want it to end.

I Liked Her Sassy

CHAPTER 21

RYKER

This wasn't my plan. I'd even sworn to myself I would wait until the end of our date to touch her. I knew touching her would lead to kissing her. Seeing that bare shoulder with those fucking adorable freckles the moment she walked out of her door tonight had made me want to kiss her. It was a miracle I'd made it this long. Seeing her study my lips like she wanted to lick them had been my undoing. I knew I had good lips. Females had talked about my lips most of my life. Aurora's fixed gaze on them, and the desire in her expression had been too much for me. I was weak where she was concerned. If she wanted to nibble on my damn lips, she could. I was sure I'd let her do anything she asked.

Hell, I didn't know what this feeling was or what was happening. I just wanted to be with her all the time. She'd wanted to feel my laughter. Her explaining that to me had made my chest ache in an unfamiliar way. I wanted to laugh so she could feel it, but damn—nothing felt funny right now.

Another soft moan came from her, and I knew I had to stop this before I couldn't. I was going to respect her, like I'd promised. I knew she was innocent, just like I knew she had no idea she was making the sexy little sounds that were going straight past my heart and good sense to a much lower region she knew nothing about.

Stopping was going to be like taking my arm and ripping it from my body. Her other hand came up to touch my chest. Her right hand fisted, and she had my T-shirt in her grip. She was holding on to me as if she could read my mind and knew I was battling with my desire for her and being a good guy. She tasted like honey and smelled like coconut. I couldn't get enough of it. No one should taste and smell this good. It was unfair.

I reached deep and grabbed every ounce of self-control inside me before pressing one last kiss to her lips. She hadn't expected the abrupt ending, and the confused look in her dazed eyes just about broke my resolve. I inhaled deeply, bent my head, and pressed my lips to her bare shoulder, taking in the softness of her skin for the briefest moment;

then I let her go and stepped away. Needing to get enough space so her smell wasn't fighting with my willpower.

"That..." I paused. I needed to be sure how I explained this. I wasn't clearheaded enough just yet for talking. Taking a few deep, slow breaths, I tried again. "That was amazing. But I didn't bring you here to do that. I have to stop while I can." I added the last sentence, realizing she needed it spelled out for her. As much as I needed to stop that, I also wanted her to know I didn't want to.

Her eyes widened, and damn if there wasn't a flash of want in those green depths that made me groan with frustration. I was glad she couldn't hear me. She would never know this was the hardest thing I'd ever done. Someone needed to give me a goddamn award. Beer would be good right now.

"We need to eat," I blurted out, and had to stop looking at her swollen pink lips and flushed cheeks before we ended up on the sofa. I wasn't a saint. Although, at the moment, I was feeling saintlike.

I moved to the bar and grabbed a plate, anything to keep from touching her again. I turned to hand it to her. She was still standing in the same spot, watching me. Slowly she walked over to take the plate, and a small smile touched her lips as she reached out for it. It didn't reach her eyes, and I could tell it was forced. Shit. I was not doing this right. I didn't let her take the plate. I set it back down and mentally slapped myself for making a mess of this. Tonight wasn't supposed to go this way.

I started to reach out and touch her arm but stopped myself. The way she felt, getting her too close meant I'd smell her again. Not a good idea. "You look upset. I didn't stop the kissing because I wasn't enjoying it or didn't want to. You . . . or touching you." I was stumbling with my words again, and it was so damn frustrating. She was struggling to read my lips. I could see it in her expression. I focused on her face and slowed down my rambling.

"I want you, Aurora. In every way. More than I have ever wanted anything in my life. I want to be near you, talk to you, see you smile, get to know all about you, what kind of pizza to order you, what your favorite drink is, all of it. I want all of it. But I also want to lay you down on that sofa over there and cover you with my body. I'm not going to. Not tonight. I want to do this right with you. You're important to me."

I'd said that all as slowly and clearly as I could instead of just letting my thoughts fall as they came and confusing her. I still wasn't sure if I'd been talking slow enough for her to follow. Maybe I needed to text it to her. Her eyes stopped studying my lips when she was sure I was done talking, and she lifted her gaze to meet mine. We stood there for a moment without words. The only sound I heard was our breathing, which was slowing as we calmed down from the mutual attraction.

"I like bacon on my pizza and thick crust. I drink water most of the time, but I love Cherry Coke." The corners of her lips lifted slowly after she said it, and her eyes twinkled, matching the teasing grin that had spread across her lips. Jesus, I was sunk. It had happened that quick. That easy.

"Where did you learn to play pool?" I asked her, liking the lightness of her mood.

She pressed her lips together then to keep from laughing, and I wished she wouldn't do that. I wanted to hear her laugh. She was still holding back on me there. "Dad. He bought us a pool table for Christmas when I was five. When they moved, he left it. I would play when I was missing Hunter."

I had a feeling those memories weren't good ones. She wasn't frowning, but I could imagine her dad moving out and taking her twin brother with him had been hard on her. Not only was the man a bigot, he was selfish. Both parents were selfish, for that matter. They hadn't been thinking about Aurora and Hunter. Their children's needs hadn't come first.

"Let's eat, then I'll see just how good you are."

The cocky, self-assured grin made me want to grab her and kiss her some more.

She closed the space between us, and I tensed, trying to make a quick decision, when she reached around me and took the plate I had set back down. Then she winked at me before turning her attention to the pizza. I stood there grinning like a damn fool. I liked her sassy. No, I fucking loved it.

She took two pieces of the meat pizza. I went to the fridge and grabbed her a bottle of water since there was no Cherry Coke. Although there would be next time. I'd be sure of it. Then I took a beer out for me. When I closed the fridge, I looked back at her sitting on the barstool, and it hit me I was driving her home tonight. This was all new to me. I had to make smarter decisions. To think of someone other than myself. I wanted to be better. I'd never cared about what anyone thought of me. I had always been living my life and doing it my way. Not anymore.

I opened the fridge again and put the beer back, then grabbed a second bottle of water. When I closed the fridge this time, I was smiling. Turning to see her watching me now, I liked how she made me feel.

"If you didn't have to drive me home, I wouldn't care if you drank the beer," she said. I hadn't realized she'd caught me. "Do Nash's parents not look in the fridge?"

"Not yet they haven't. Nash has gotten away with a lot this year, though. His accident changed things," I replied, and walked over to her to place both our waters on the bar. I grabbed a plate and put two slices of each pizza on my plate along with some wings, then stuck a piece of the cheese bread in my mouth before sitting back down.

I felt her gaze on me. I turned my head to see her smiling so big I was expecting that laugh I was still waiting to hear. I bit off the cheese bread that was in my mouth and began to chew while holding the other half in my hand. She watched me, and I watched her watching me.

When I finally swallowed, I asked, "What?" not minding her watching me in the least.

"I just liked watching you eat," she said.

I nodded my head to the plate in front of her. "I want to see you eat too."

Then there it was . . . she laughed. A real laugh and it was adorable. The best part was she didn't even realize she'd done it. She was comfortable with me. I wasn't the only one enjoying myself. This was mutual.

I Missed You

CHAPTER 22

AURORA

"By the smile on your face I'm guessing last night was fun," Hunter signed to me when I walked into the kitchen the next morning to get my waffle.

"Yes," I replied with my voice.

Hunter gave a nod. "Good." He said the word, but his frown didn't match what he was saying. I assumed he had hoped I would have decided I didn't like Ryker.

"I'm going to tell Dad about Ryker," I said.

Hunter shook his head no at me. His eyes flared with panic. That made my anger toward my father spike even more. I hated how Hunter feared standing up to him.

"Yes," I told him before he could argue. "I don't want to keep him a secret. It's not fair."

Hunter ran a hand over his face as if he was trying to think this through and needed a moment. I knew before I'd arrived that there was no conflict in this house. Hunter didn't like conflict. He never had. If he'd been more like me, then I wondered if he would even be playing football now. Had that been forced upon him, or did he love the sport like he appeared to? He knew nothing else.

"Could you at least wait until the game is over Friday night? We don't need anything distracting us."

I started to say no, then paused and wondered if maybe I was being selfish about telling Dad. Hunter and Ryker both needed to win this playoff game. If Dad was going to fight me on this, then his attention would either be taken off Hunter for once, or he'd take it out on Hunter, and I didn't want Hunter to have more pressure on him from Dad than he already did. There was also the fact that it would distract Ryker with my drama, and he didn't need that. Hunter and Ryker didn't need me standing between them at the moment. Dad would expect Hunter to overcome all of that and win the game. This could all go so many different ways I couldn't gamble on it.

"Tomorrow night. Let us get through tomorrow night. If we win, and we should, then let's talk about it before you decide to tell Dad. We could win State, and you know that will secure me getting a football scholarship."

He was talking and signing. The anxiety clear in his movements and expression. I was right in my assumption that Dad would make his life even harder. Hunter didn't want to experience that, and I didn't blame him. But one day soon he was going to have to tell our father no and be his own man.

"Okay," I agreed. Although Hunter already had scholarship offers from colleges. He wasn't happy with any of them, or our father wasn't happy about any of them yet. Maybe Hunter would make his own decision about where he went. I wished he would. Then I thought of Ryker and any offers he might have or where he wanted to go. Would it be far away?

Hunter sighed, and we stood there not speaking, moving, or eating. I wasn't that hungry anymore. But I would be starving before lunch. I began to move toward the box of frozen waffles still on the counter. Going through the motions of toasting one and putting the box up, I wondered if we were making a bigger deal out of all this than was necessary. I knew Dad was controlling. I just didn't know if this was really going to be an issue for him. I was going by Hunter's word.

When my waffle popped up, I grabbed it with a napkin so as not to burn my fingers, then turned to get a bottle of water from the fridge. I knew Hunter was still standing in the same place. He hadn't moved. He was waiting on me to look at him again. Which meant he had more to say. I thought about walking outside to his truck, but that would have been rude.

I took a bite of the waffle and gave him my attention.

He shook his head and then laughed, but it didn't look like a real laugh. One of disbelief or frustration. If I could hear, I imagined it would have been hard or maybe cold. "How did one week change so much? Last week my only concern had been the field. Winning." He walked off then. Toward the front door.

He hadn't said it, but he blamed me. For coming here and making things hard on him. I knew he wanted me to be interested in anyone else other than Ryker. I hadn't thought I would come here and meet someone like Ryker. It had been so quick. Happened so fast. I couldn't help but fear it would end as quickly as it had started.

Following him to the truck, I tried not to worry. I wanted to think about how Ryker made me smile. How I felt being around him. The excitement I didn't know existed. But this all had been fast. I hadn't even known him last week. Now he was all I thought about. Was that bad? When the new wore off for him, would he move on to someone else? Was I being naive?

Probably.

Possibly.

By the time we arrived at school, I had been set on not being the silly girl waiting on the guy. I wouldn't look for Ryker. If he was there, then great. If he wasn't, I was secure with myself. I had this all under control. I had pep-talked myself up and was so focused on not being obsessed with Ryker that I swung open my door, refusing to look around the parking lot for him, and climbed down out of the truck only to slam straight into his broad chest.

I made a sound as his hands grabbed my waist to steady me, and I felt the vibration in his chest as he said something. Lifting my head to stare into the eyes that looked like a dark, warm liquid I could easily drown in and enjoy it, I knew my pep talk was pointless. All it took was one look at him, and I didn't seem to care about anything else. This had to be dangerous for my heart. I cared too much and way too quickly.

"Are you okay?" he asked, his beautiful eyes searching my face for answers to my weird, almost frantic exit of my brother's truck.

I nodded. His hands stayed on my waist. For a moment I thought he was going to kiss me. Right here in front of Hunter and the rest of the parking lot. Lost in his gaze, I didn't care who saw us. Nothing else mattered.

"You sure?" he asked, and again I was transfixed on the perfect fullness of his lips. I watched them more closely than was necessary.

"Yes. I was just distracted," I replied, using my voice.

He grinned then. When I used my voice with him, he liked it. I could always see the pleasure on his face. That was unique for me. When I was younger and used my voice with the hearing who weren't my family, I'd gotten mixed reactions. Most people were uncomfortable with it. They didn't like the way it sounded, and I could tell. I'd stopped speaking except to my family or teachers.

Ryker didn't react the way the others had, though. He wanted to hear me. I wondered if it was the same for him as me wanting to feel his laughter last night.

His hands moved from my waist, and he took a step back. I wanted to protest, but before I could react at all, he began to use his hands. It was slow and unsure, but he clearly signed, "I missed you."

I stared at his hands for a moment longer, then lifted my eyes to his face. I didn't know what to say. I was surprised, and an odd feeling of emotion came over me.

"Did I do it correctly?" he asked then with worry creasing his forehead.

I nodded. "I missed you too," I signed back to him.

The smile that broke across his face as he understood what I had signed lit up my world. My eyes burned with the emotion growing thicker inside my throat as it tightened. He had signed. He had taken the time to learn to say something to me in the way that was easiest for me. I was going to cry and look like an idiot. Swallowing hard, I bit my bottom lip to keep from embarrassing myself with the tears threatening to spill.

He took a quick, determined breath, then again lifted his hands and signed, "Good morning."

I smiled, and the expression was a watery one. I was failing at the not-crying thing. I signed back, "Good morning," then wiped at the stray tear breaking free. All that trying to convince myself not to care too much about him. To protect myself. We had just met this week. He could move on to someone else tomorrow. Then this. He showed up this morning and greeted me with sign language. How did anyone think he was a bad guy?

"Why are you crying?" he asked with his words this time. Then reached out to touch my cheek. He was unsure now. The smile gone. He turned his head from me and I followed his gaze to see Hunter standing there. I'd forgotten about Hunter, and the rest of the world for that matter.

All I caught from my brother was "that." I didn't know what he'd been saying to Ryker.

Ryker's hand moved from my face to my shoulders as he pulled me to his side. It wasn't a possessive move, or it didn't feel that way. It was more protective. He was gentle. He reached around and slid my backpack off my other shoulder then moved it to his. Our eyes met, and I dropped my gaze to his mouth to see if he wanted to say something.

"I'd do anything for you," he said simply.

There was the lump in my throat again. I didn't know what my brother had said to him, but this was his response. Hunter had walked toward the school, leaving us alone.

"Why?" I asked him, needing to understand how I had become this important to him so quickly. I had decided I'd come to care about him so much because he was the first guy who had made me feel this way. I was inexperienced with guys.

"Being with you makes me feel right. Complete."

Another tear escaped, and his thumb brushed it away before he kissed my cheek where it had been. The warmth of his breath made me shiver and move into him, wishing I could stay like this beside him forever.

I'd never hated first period more in my life.

Calm the Hell Down
CHAPTER 23

RYKER

"I spent breakfast trying to convince her that dating you was making things difficult for the team. I need her to keep you a secret until tomorrow. Our roles in this game are crucial. You know this. I don't trust my dad's reaction to her dating you. If this shit blows up in our face before Friday, then our heads won't be in the game. But you signing to her . . . I wasn't expecting that." Hunter's words stayed with me all morning.

It was a seal of approval I hadn't expected to get from Hunter Maclay. I'd had to stay to talk to the teacher, who wanted to discuss my last test grade, after first period, so I'd missed seeing Aurora between classes. Even if seeing her always made me late to my next class. Nash was beside me as soon as second period ended.

"In case you missed it, Nova was all over Brett in the hall this morning," he said as if to warn me.

"Good," I replied, thinking it was a relief, and I hoped the tennis player could keep her interested for a long while.

"You don't care?" he asked.

"Hell no. Helps me out."

"Gets his attention off Tallulah, so I was fucking thrilled, but then I wasn't sure where you were with this Aurora thing."

"I'm all in with it. Not interested in anyone else," I said, turning my head enough to look him in the eyes as I said it.

"Is that why you're walking in this direction instead of your third-period class? To see her?"

"Yup."

"Damn, I didn't think I'd ever see you get all tangled up over a female."

I thought about that for a moment. "Me either," I finally said. This was never something I'd expected. But the moment I'd seen her Monday, something inside me had come alive. The more I was around her, and even just texting with her, getting to know her, I was getting more attached. I had no other way to describe it.

"You ready for tomorrow night? North Bank hasn't

lost a game. Richards is the number one scouted quarter-back in the state. It's going to take all we have to pull off a win."

I had a lot more faith in Hunter than Nash did. He was on the sidelines now, coaching. He didn't feel the vibe on the field anymore. Only the team could know for sure if we had this. After Hunter's approval today, I knew we were good. His head would be back on the field. That's all we needed.

"We're ready," I told him. I didn't have time to talk any more about it, because Aurora stepped through the crowd in the hallway, and her eyes met mine. The way her face lit up at the sight of me made me feel like a fuck-ing god. "Gotta go," I said to Nash, and moved with ease through the bodies blocking my way, since I was larger than most of them.

She didn't have to move, because I was to her in moments. I'd spent most of last period watching the same YouTube video I'd studied last night on sign language for beginners. I was ready to try what I had learned. Even though I'd only watched it over and over on my phone, which I had hidden in my book, and not actually tried it yet.

"How has your day been?" I signed, hoping I'd done it correctly. This morning I had been a little more confident.

I'd practiced the movements late into the night and all morning in the mirror. This time I wasn't as prepared.

She beamed at me and signed her reply, but spoke the words as she did it. "Better now."

"Mine too," I replied, not knowing the sign for that or anything more.

I'd give anything to get to go with her to all her classes. See her all day. Instead we had nothing together.

I reached and took her backpack from her shoulder and slipped it over mine before nodding my head in the direction of her next class. "I'll walk you to your class," I said to her. She gave me a pleased grin.

I slid a hand around her back and moved her through the people with ease. She was small, but against me it was easier to get by as everyone rushed to their classes when the three-minute-warning bell went off. I'd be late, but I wasn't worried.

Her classroom door was open, and as others hurried inside, I reluctantly took her bag and gave it back to her. I signed, "I miss you." Because I already did.

She signed, "I miss you too."

I fought the urge to kiss her and watched as she went into the room.

When I turned to leave, there was Nova. She had one eyebrow raised, and her left hand rested on her hip. "Did you just use sign language?" she asked incredulously.

I saw no reason to answer her, but I nodded before walking past her and toward my classroom.

"I'm seeing someone else now. I'm not playing your games. You can stop acting like an ass. It didn't work," she called out to me.

I once again nodded and kept walking.

The late bell rang just as I stepped into my classroom.

Lunch with Aurora was difficult. Everyone was talking loudly. Even Nash was focused on the game tomorrow night. Hunter didn't watch us the entire time, which was a relief, since I just wanted to talk to Aurora. But with all the activity and interruptions, it made things hard. When someone at the table would ask me a question or direct the attention toward me, answering them meant turning my head away from Aurora, and she had no idea what was being said. I didn't like her being isolated like that. There had to be a better way to do lunch. It was the only time I had with her during the day.

I kept her hand in mine under the table as much as I could. It gave me some connection to her, even if we barely got to talk without being interrupted. Tallulah sat down across from us, and she signed with Aurora, which meant I had to let go of her hand, and I was torn between being frustrated with Tallulah and grateful to her for making Aurora feel included.

I watched them sign, trying to figure out anything I might recognize and learn. Tallulah saw me and began using words as she signed, for my benefit. The guys would try and draw me back into the conversation often, and I had to settle on placing my hand on Aurora's thigh. When I had placed it there at first, she jumped a little, and I'd grinned at her. The pink tint to her cheeks made me want to kiss her, but then again, it didn't take much to make me want to kiss her.

The bell ringing and ending lunch was frustrating. This had been too short. I'd have practice this afternoon, and Aurora had two tests tomorrow she had to study for tonight after dinner with her family. This was all I'd get to see of her today. There was no time between our next periods for me to see her. I took her hand as we stood and walked slowly behind everyone else to leave the cafeteria.

Letting her hand go so she could walk away from me was harder than it should have been. When I couldn't see her any longer, I turned and headed to my next class. Asa was standing between me and the class.

"You're really into her." He wasn't asking me. He was just noting it.

"Yeah, I am," I replied anyway.

He shrugged. "She's something to look at, but the deaf thing seems like too much work."

I knew Asa well enough to know he wasn't being an ass. He was just too blunt. Said things without thinking. But hearing him say it as if that made her defective infuriated me. Anger crawled up my spine and exploded before I could think clearly.

Then I was in front of him, and he was shoved up against the lockers behind him. My head was pounding and my blood pumping. I knew I had to get control of myself, but it was like I'd stepped away and was watching this from afar, unable to do anything about it.

"Don't you ever fucking talk about her like that again!" The roar of my voice carried down the hallway. I was aware of it, but I was detached.

"Jesus, man! I wasn't bashing her. Calm the hell down," Asa said just as angrily, his eyes wide with shock.

"She's goddamn perfect. Do you understand me? Don't ever say something like that about her again!" I was still yelling.

The hands that grabbed my shoulders were firm and strong. I was hauled backward off Asa, and it was that moment I managed to come back to myself and snap out of whatever had taken over me.

"My office. Both of you." Principal Haswell's firm voice

was not coming from behind me but from a distance away. I jerked my head back to see who had pulled me off Asa, and I found Coach's pissed-off expression as he shoved me toward Haswell with enough force that I stumbled at first.

I didn't know what to expect. I'd never snapped like that before. I couldn't explain it. Asa walked beside me, but he kept a distance. I knew Coach was behind us as we made our way to Haswell's office.

Tomorrow night could be the game that solidified my college education. It was important. I wanted to play football four more years in college, but I also knew my parents really wanted me to get a scholarship. I hadn't thought about any of that, though, when I'd snapped on Asa. Without a scholarship to a big university, I'd be going somewhere more affordable. This game would be what decided it all. Now there was a good chance I wouldn't be playing in it.

We Have a Game to Win
CHAPTER 24

AURORA

I wasn't sure if I was being paranoid or what was happening, but as I walked out to find Ella in the parking lot after school, it felt like everyone was looking at me. Other than the first day I was here, I hadn't felt this way. The new had quickly worn off, or Ryker's presence beside me had stopped it.

Either way, when I finally got to Ella's car, I was relieved to close the door behind me and get away from it. It had been an odd feeling. One I didn't like in the least.

I looked at Ella and smiled. Talking to her was always awkward. She made it that way.

She said hello, and although I couldn't hear, I could

tell she was talking loudly by her wide eyes and the over-exaggeration of her mouth. She did that a lot with me. I'd seen my dad and brother both tell her that yelling at me didn't help. She wasn't the brightest person I'd ever met, though. It wasn't sinking in that yelling at me wasn't required.

Hello, I replied silently.

That was enough conversation for her, and she was now happily pulling away from the line of cars picking up students and driving away. I sighed with relief. This afternoon had been long. No Ryker after lunch and I understood why, but I missed him.

Tonight we would eat a very healthy, unappetizing meal that Ella would prepare, and Dad would talk about tomorrow's game with Hunter while we ate. Then I had to study for a Literature test I wasn't too worried about and a Trig test that did concern me some.

The ride home was nothing new, and my afternoon went as planned. It wasn't until dinner that things took a bad turn. Hunter came into my room abruptly, the door swinging open wide and a look of anger on his face. I jumped up, startled at his sudden appearance, but then I quickly became annoyed with his bursting in like this.

"I warned you," he signed. "I knew this was bad. I asked you for one thing. One simple thing. Playoffs are what will determine my college career. Thanks to Ryker, winning tomorrow night is going to be impossible." He signed all of it. His anger also verging on fear that flashed in his eyes.

"What happened?" I asked, confused.

"You. You happened. Ryker attacked Asa in the hallway over some comment he made about you. They spent the afternoon in Haswell's office with Coach Rich. The decision was to let Asa play, since he hadn't meant to say anything offensive, but Ryker has to sit out the first half of the game. Do you have any idea what could happen to us without Ryker the first half?" He threw his hands up in the air then with frustration.

"This is Ryker's future too. He will go to the college that gives him a full scholarship. He has the makings to be great in college and could go pro. But he's so wrapped up in you this week that he's tossing that away over Asa saying something about you being deaf." Hunter dropped his hands to his side. He was done signing. I didn't see how this was my fault, though.

"What did Asa say?" I asked, needing to understand why Ryker had attacked him. And what exactly did *attack* mean? Did he throw a punch?

Hunter looked annoyed, but I could see by the way his expression changed that he wasn't mad at Ryker. He needed to be mad at someone, so he was directing it at me. Making this all my fault. Even when he knew it wasn't. "Asa said something about it being hard to talk to you since you're deaf. Not sure exactly how it was put, but Ryker reacted more violently than necessary." He paused a minute and ran a hand over his face. Then he said, "I understand, though. His reaction. His wanting to defend or protect you—I respect him for it. But damn, Aurora. We have a game to win. Ryker is my best receiver."

"What did Ryker do? Hit him?" I hoped not. This all seemed a bit much. It was true I was deaf, and yes, communicating with me for Ryker was a challenge.

"Slammed him against the lockers and threatened him. Nothing too severe, but it was hands-on and aggressive. Coach stopped him. It could have been worse. But Asa was trying to calm Ryker down, not make him angrier." Hunter shook his head then and tilted it back to stare up at the ceiling.

Asa wasn't small. But Ryker was a little larger, I guessed. I couldn't see him being strong enough to slam Asa against the lockers, though. The image bothered me. That wasn't much to get upset about, and the truth was, the more time Ryker spent with me the more people were going to talk. They would say much worse things. He couldn't react that way every time or ever again. Hunter was right; he had a future to worry about. The reality of this situation was starting to sink in. I hadn't considered something like this could happen.

"More people will say things. He has to accept that and not defend you unless it's absolutely crucial. He can't do this every time someone says something about you being deaf."

He was only saying exactly what I was thinking. I agreed, but I didn't know what to do now. How to handle it.

"Dad will want to know about what happened. Ryker won't be playing first half, and I need to tell him why. I am not going to tell him you are talking to Ryker or seeing him. Just that Ryker took offense to it for my sake."

This would happen at dinner. I had to go along with it, but I hated the lie. I wanted to tell Dad about Ryker. Hiding him was wrong, especially for the reasons I was having to do so. Skin color was not important. My father was an educated man, and I would hope he believed that too. Hunter didn't think so. Hunter also knew our father much better than I did.

I studied my brother's expression for a moment, wondering if he was right. Would telling Dad the truth only cause more issues? I could wait. One more day. The game was tomorrow night, and Hunter was already worried about playing without Ryker.

I just nodded. I would go along with whatever he told Dad at dinner.

Hunter turned to leave my room, and I saw my phone light up where I had left it in the center of my bed. I hurried over to it and picked it up to see two text messages from Ryker. And one from Tallulah.

I went to Ryker's text first.

We need to talk. Can I see you tonight?

Then the next one, two minutes after the first

Don't let Hunter convince you of anything please. Let me explain.

Before responding, I went to Tallulah's text.

Do you want to ride with me to the game tomorrow? We can sit together.

That one I had an immediate answer for, so I responded.

Yes. Thank you!

Then I went back to Ryker's text. Keeping my distance from him until the game was over might be best, but it wasn't fair. Not to him. I wanted to see him. To tell him that defending me when someone states the obvious has to stop.

Can you pick me up outside at 8:30?

His immediate response was:

Yes!

I smiled in spite of it all. He always made me smile.

She Must Be Something Special
CHAPTER 25

RYKER

I stood in the kitchen, where I had been summoned by my father the moment I walked into the house. My sister was nowhere in sight, which meant he'd sent her to her room for this. Nahla loved gossip, and she was nosy as hell. She'd be listening from the hallway.

Mom was cooking something on the stove, and she glanced back at me with a concerned expression before stirring what had to be chili in that large pot, because she didn't cook much else in it. Concerned over the fact my mother was cooking, I moved my gaze to my dad. He was standing with his arms crossed over his chest, leaning on the counter, studying me hard.

"Explain this bullshit," he said, then pointed to the kitchen table for me to sit down. If he wasn't sitting, then I was going to stand too. He liked to tower over us when we were in trouble, but now that I was big enough to look him in the eyes he wanted me to sit. Nope.

"Asa was out of line. He needs to watch his dumbass mouth. I corrected him." I knew he already had the details from Coach Rich. This was pointless. He just wanted to know why I cared about Asa saying anything about Aurora.

"You like the Maclay girl?" he asked, his tone even. No angry edge to it.

"Yes. I do."

Mom turned around again to look at me. I flicked my eyes toward her a moment, then back to my father. She looked even more concerned now, and I didn't see why she should.

"She's deaf. You don't know sign language. It would be hard to communicate with her. That is what Asa was saying, from my understanding of the situation. That was out of line? He needed to be slammed against a locker and threatened because he was pointing out the truth?"

I tensed. "It was the way he said it. The tone in his voice," I replied, unable not to sound pissed.

"His tone? You slammed not only a friend, but a team-mate, against the motherfucking locker because of his tone?

Your future depends on this game, son. Not playing in it for the entire first half draws attention. The bad kind. You think scouts won't find out why you aren't playing? You think they want to bring a guy in with a fucking hot head that snaps over stupid shit?"

"It wasn't stupid." I stopped him and realized I'd taken a step in his direction.

His eyebrows shot up at my movement. I may have been his height, and my shoulders were wide for my age, but his were wider. He was where I got my size from, but my biceps weren't as large as his.

"Ryker." My mother's voice warned me, almost panicked.

"She's making you stupid. Shit. This is a first," Dad said, then shook his head in disbelief. "Boy, you got a college career to focus on. You want to get out of this town and be someone, you have the talent and size to do it. But a girl making you act like an idiot will stop that. End it all."

"Aurora understands all this. Hell, her brother is the most driven athlete I've ever known. It's all he fucking does. She gets this is important to my future. She won't try and stand in my way."

Dad poked my chest with his large finger. "You. It's you that will sink it. Because of her. Football comes first.

Before females. You've always known that. Don't let this
one mess up your head. Your goals."

"She isn't," I shot back at him.

"She did today. And she didn't even mean to."

I knew my reaction to Asa was a mistake. I wasn't
going to admit it, but I knew it. I'd snapped and couldn't
seem to stop myself. My need to protect her had been controlling me. The fact someone could say something much
worse eventually wasn't lost on me. I didn't know if I
could stop myself from reacting to it. Today I hadn't been
able to.

"Honey, we want you to have relationships. You're
young, and the fact you like this girl so much makes me
happy. It gives me hope that you're maturing in that regard.
But your father is right. You have to think about your
future first. You can't let that hot head of yours pop off
over everything someone says about her." My mom had
moved closer, and Dad knew as well as I did she was moving in to protect me, if needed. Dad had never been abusive
or anything like that, but I had also never stood up to him
like I had a moment ago.

"There is also one more thing. I don't know if you
have thought about yet. She's white." Dad said it as if this
was a big deal. I'd dated plenty of white girls. Hell, my
aunt was white.

"So," I said, incredulous that he'd even brought up skin color.

"Coach Rich mentioned her daddy might have an issue with it when I talked to him today. Something Hunter said to him about not saying anything to his dad about this. He wanted to explain it to him."

Shit. I hadn't thought about her dad finding out. Aurora hadn't mentioned it when I'd texted her. But Hunter had already made it clear my being black was going to be an issue with his dad.

"Aurora doesn't agree with Hunter on how her dad is gonna react. But his opinion is not a concern to her. Don't see why it should be for you," I said.

He laughed then but it wasn't one full of humor, either. I was the one that said, "You're a stupid fuck." My hands balled into fists I would never use on my dad, so they stayed by my side.

"If that girl's daddy don't want her dating a black man, then she won't. He'll lock her ass up. Have you seen the way he controls his son? The man stands on the sidelines and tells Hunter what to do. The boy obeys like a damn robot. If I yelled at you like that, we'd end up tied up on the damn football field, because your strong-willed ass would smart off. Hunter does what he's told to do by that man, and it ain't healthy. You think he won't do the same with his daughter?"

"She won't let him. You don't know her. You haven't met her. She is nothing like Hunter. The first night I got to spend time with her was because her dad had pissed her off and she left the house. After texting me to come get her. She makes her own choices."

"How do you talk to her?" my mother interrupted. I turned my gaze back to her, and along with the concern, I saw curiosity. She was trying to understand. But then I expected that of my mom.

"She reads lips well, and she trusts me enough to use her voice with me. She doesn't do that with anyone else but her brother and parents. And I'm learning sign language from some YouTube videos I found. Tallulah is going to teach me more after football season, but for now I'm teaching myself a little at a time."

My mother's eyes went wide, and the proud smile on her face wiped out the concern. "You're teaching yourself to sign?" she asked, but not needing me to answer. It was more of an impressed statement. Something she wouldn't expect from me.

"Shit," my father muttered. "This girl just moved here last weekend. How the hell did you get wrapped up with her so damn fast?" He was not impressed. He was aggravated.

I knew this was all happening fast. This week felt like

it had been so much longer. I didn't like the me I had been last week. I didn't want to be him again. Because that guy didn't know what it was like to see Aurora smile and know he'd been the one to cause that.

"Monday morning, the first moment I saw her, something fell into place."

Dad groaned and hit the counter with his palm. "Well that's just fucking beautiful." He didn't sound at all happy. He was being sarcastic. "You have a college career ahead of you! Don't go getting all sappy about this girl when you have to leave her this summer."

My mom reached out and touched my arm and squeezed it gently. She didn't say anything. Dad stalked out of the kitchen without another word. When the door to his man cave closed loudly behind him, mom gave me a smile. "He'll calm down. He's just worried about you losing a chance to play SEC football. You know that." She stood on her tippy-toes, and I leaned down enough so she could kiss my cheek.

"I can't wait to meet this girl. She must be something special."

I smiled. "She is."

It Was Their Normal

CHAPTER 26

AURORA

I knew they had been discussing me when I walked into the dining room, because I saw my name on Hunter's lips. I didn't pay attention to what they were saying but went to the chair at the table that was mine. I already knew this was going to be a bad meal with a worse topic of conversation.

Ella was placing the food in the center of the table, and I recognized something that had couscous in it. That was promising if the stuff with it wasn't tofu. I couldn't be sure. Ella's last dinner had been remarkably weird as well as bad.

When Hunter sat down across from me, I looked at him instead of the food, and he gave me a silent warning. He was making sure I let him talk and hadn't decided to tell Dad the truth. For Hunter's sake and Ryker's, I wasn't going to do that tonight. He was right. The game was important for both of them.

Hunter signed and spoke at the same time. He and Dad would do that for Ella. I didn't. I wasn't using my voice with her. If it was anything they thought she needed to hear, they'd tell her. "Dad is asking you something," he said so I would turn to look at Dad. I'd been avoiding him. I didn't want to talk to him. If it wasn't for the silent pleading in Hunter's eyes, I'd have continued to ignore him. For my brother, I didn't. I turned my gaze to my dad.

"Why do you think Ryker defended you today?" he asked point-blank. Dad never was one to beat around the bush.

"He has been nice. Very helpful at school the times I've been around him. One of the few people who have tried to speak to me and get to know me." I signed then I was done. No more.

Dad frowned. "This is all friendly with him? Ryker is known to use girls. He has a new one every time I see him."

"He is being friendly. Just like Nash and Tallulah are friendly."

Dad turned his head to Hunter, and I followed with my gaze.

"That's what I told you," Hunter said to Dad. "He said

Asa's tone was what made him angry. Not that he was calling Aurora deaf. Asa can be a jerk." Hunter's expression
was neutral, but I could see the tension in his shoulders.
I wondered what Dad's voice sounded like. Was it hard?
Threatening?

I looked back to see Dad's response. "Ryker has college scouts coming to see him at this game, as do you. He
has been contacted by both Georgia and Vandy already.
I don't understand why he'd jeopardize that. His father
should have a tighter hold on the boy. So much talent and
he doesn't focus on it. He has a future in football, or he
would if he stopped with the wild life." He was speaking
to both of us.

I hadn't known he had those two colleges already talking to him. He'd never said that to me. I also didn't want to
be reminded of his wild life.

Hunter shrugged as if he was relaxed, but his body was
strung so tight I wondered how Dad didn't notice. He was
nervous. Dad always made him this way. "I don't either.
He's got a hot head at times. Asa may have made him mad
earlier, and that was just what finally set him off."

Ella took a bowl from the table that held some sort of
cucumber-and-onion salad in it and passed it to me. She
wanted us to start eating. I was done with this conversation too, and as much as I didn't want to eat this salad, I

took some then passed it to Dad. He was still frowning and looked at it, then ignored it before looking back at Hunter.

I set the bowl down, watching my dad's lips because he'd stopped signing.

"You can't let Ryker's dumb, careless attitude affect the game. This is on you now. You handle it. Get it done. Focus. Nothing else but that game matters in your world right now. Got me? Nothing. Ryker can act like a—" He stopped then, but I didn't turn my eyes away from him. He was looking at Ella now. She must have been speaking, but I didn't turn to see what she was saying. Instead I shifted my gaze to Hunter. He was watching me. When our eyes met, he lifted his eyebrows as if to make a point. He was trying to convey something to me silently. I quickly looked back at Dad to catch him saying, "My house. I'll use whatever damn word I choose." Then he picked up the bowl he'd ignored earlier.

A hand touched my arm. Ella was handing me the couscous dish now, and I was hoping this wasn't tofu. I got some of it, then handed it reluctantly to Dad. I wanted to leave this table. I wanted to ask Hunter what was said that I'd missed. Dad took the bowl this time; he glanced at it then up at Ella. "Is this tofu?" he asked. The creases on his forehead were permanent from years of frowning, but when he was scowling, they were worse. He hated tofu as much as I did. It was possibly the only thing we had in common.

I quickly looked to catch Ella's response. She nodded and said, "Yes, but I did something different to it. Just try it."

Yuck.

She handed me the final thing she'd brought to the table. It was a bread of some sort. Lots of seeds or nuts and it was brown. Dark brown. If we had real butter to go on this, it would be good. I knew, however, that the butter look-alike on the table was from the health food store and disgusting. I'd given it a try before on my waffle. There was real butter in the fridge. Why couldn't she just let us use that?

I handed the bread to Dad, who then said, "Where's the real butter?"

Ella walked out of the room with an annoyed expression. She wasn't as willing to please him as Hunter was. I doubted he was as hard on her as he was on Hunter. It took her a moment to come back, and I began to wonder if she had left. As much as I wanted butter, that would be what he deserved. Ella had made the meal; he could have gone to get the butter himself. Maybe thanked her for the meal. She did return with the butter, though. The meal went on with no more talk of Ryker. Dad didn't seem to care about Ella's feelings and went right back to talking about the game with

Hunter. Whenever I looked up, Hunter would be nodding and Dad would be talking. Every move Hunter could possibly make on the field was being gone over. I felt bad for Hunter, but he let Dad do this to him. I just didn't understand why. Why didn't he stand up to the man?

When we were all as finished as we were going to be, because Hunter and I had struggled to eat the dinner but tried our best to get most of it down, I helped Ella clean the table and kitchen. Dad expected us to do it. We were females. If I didn't feel bad about Ella doing it herself, I'd leave. But it wasn't her fault. Dad told Hunter to come with him to his office downstairs. They were going to go over the game tapes now. Did this ever get to be too much for Hunter? I was tired thinking about all he had to listen to.

It couldn't have been more perfect for me, though. While they were down in Dad's office, Ella would go up to take her long bath with a book, and I would be free to sneak out. The last thing anyone except Hunter would do would be to come check on me.

I'm leaving my house now.

The text came from Ryker. Smiling, I waited five minutes, then went quietly out the front door and headed to the road. It was 8:27 when he pulled up to the side of the road across from my house with his headlights off. I ran over to him and saw him get out to meet me at the passenger-side door. His truck was higher off the ground than Hunter's. Ryker seemed to think he had to always help me up. He took my hand, and I used it to boost myself into the truck. We didn't speak since we were in a hurry to get away without being caught by my dad. Ryker was back in the truck and turning around in the neighbor's driveway within seconds. We then headed toward town.

It was dark, and we couldn't talk while he drove. His hand reached over, and his large one took my much smaller one in his. The pleasure from a simple touch made everything that was wrong right. My dad, the game, everything. This was worth it. Feeling this way. Being with him.

He drove past the turn for town and toward the road we had taken to the field. Instead of going farther down the dirt road, he stopped at a house. Lights were on inside. A silver Toyota and a red SUV were parked in the driveway. He put his truck in park, then turned to look at me as he turned the light on so I could see his face clearly. He then signed, "This is my house."

He'd learned something new in sign language, and I was smiling so big I had to lick my lips when the stretch made their dryness obvious.

He grinned, pleased he'd done it correctly. He then said with his words, "I'd like to introduce you to my family. Then we could go to the den and talk. Mom won't let us go

to my room. Even if I'm eighteen and moving out this summer. In her house, it's her rules."

I panicked. He wanted to introduce me to his parents. I
wasn't expecting that. He also had a sister, Nahla. I remembered him telling me about her while texting one night.
What if they didn't like me, or my being deaf was weird for
them? Ella was so awkward with me still. Did they know I
was coming inside? Was he going to just surprise them with
me? Oh God.

"It's okay. You went pale," he said, squeezing my hand,
then lacing my fingers with his to bring my hand to his lips.
After he kissed it, I sighed and relaxed a little. Not completely, but a little. "My mom is excited to meet you. I don't
bring girls home. She is happy I want to bring you here.
Dad also wants to meet you, as does Nahla. She's annoying
and eleven. I apologize in advance." He said all this with a
smile in his eyes.

I took a deep, slow breath, then nodded. "Okay." I
used my voice. I had to decide now how to handle talking to them. They didn't sign, and although Ryker was trying, he didn't know nearly enough to be our go-between.
I couldn't trust they could read lips. It wasn't something
that was easy for most people. Writing or texting would be
awkward.

All I knew to do was read their lips and use my voice.

That made me so nervous my stomach knotted up. Ryker was what mattered, and I used my voice with him. He was okay with it. He said he liked it. If he liked it, then I should be okay using it with his family. Right?

Ryker leaned over and pressed a kiss to my lips. I felt his breath against my skin, and I knew he'd whispered something, although I had no idea what it was. He had to have been talking to himself. When he leaned back, he winked at me. "Let me get your door. My momma is probably watching from the window, and if she sees you get out of this truck without my help, she'll chew my ass about it later."

I laughed, then nodded. He ran around the front of the truck and was opening my door within a matter of seconds. I had hoped it would take longer and give me a moment to prepare for this. He wanted me here, and I wanted his family to like me. I had to make this as comfortable for them as I could. Talking was all I knew to do to ease them. It was their normal, and people were only at ease with their normal. That was something I knew all too well.

CHAPTER 27

RYKER

I held her hand firmly in mine, and the slight tremble of her body as I opened the door to the house told me she was nervous. I didn't want her to be. I hated that she was so worked up about meeting my family. But I wanted them to see why she was so important to me. How I'd gotten so attached to her so quickly. This would help both my parents understand my feelings for her. At least that was my hope.

Mom met us as we walked into the living room. She was smiling, and I could already tell by her expression she understood the physical attraction. Aurora was beautiful, and I didn't think she had a clue just how stunning she was.

I'd be lying if I said her looks hadn't been what had caught my attention first.

"Hello," my mom said, glancing at me for approval of her speaking, then back to Aurora. I'd assured them all Aurora could read their lips just fine. I wasn't sure, though, how Aurora was going to communicate back. Shit. I hadn't even thought about that. Before I could ask her if she wanted a piece of paper or something, she spoke.

"Hello, it's nice to meet you." I was sure my heart squeezed, because there was no other explanation for the feeling inside my chest at the sound of her voice. She didn't like using her voice, and the trust she was displaying right now shocked me speechless.

My mother's grin was something I noticed but couldn't focus on at the moment. She was pleased too. She hadn't been expecting her to talk either. Although I didn't think she understood the huge deal this was. Or the gift she was being given.

"Ryker has told us a lot about you. I'm so pleased he brought you here. Can I get you something to drink?" Mom was talking slower than normal, and I was thankful for that, because my momma could rattle off so fast it was hard to understand her sometimes, and I could hear just fine.

"Thank you for having me over, and yes, some water please," Aurora replied. At her words my mother was completely relaxed now and extremely pleased. She'd been prepared for something difficult. Aurora was making it easy for her, and if my mother hadn't been in the room with us, I would have grabbed her and kissed her.

Mom started to turn to go get the water, and I called out, "Cherry Coke. There is a bottle of it on the bottom shelf. I hid it behind the unidentified butter container yesterday. It's her favorite," I explained.

I glanced down at Aurora, who was looking up at my mouth, and when her mouth curved up at the corners, I knew she'd understood most of what I had said.

Mom didn't say anything else, but neither of us was looking at her. The pleased twinkle in Aurora's eyes made me want to go buy all the damn Cherry Coke in the state of Alabama. I'd grabbed it when I got gas yesterday, thinking I wanted to have her over soon. Now I was thinking I should have been giving her Cherry Coke every day. Greeting her with it at school in the mornings.

"I want her hair." Nahla's voice interrupted us, and I lifted my gaze to see my sister coming in the door from the hallway. "Seriously, I wish I was white just so I could have that hair."

I smirked and gave a shake of my head before placing my hand on Aurora's waist and turning her to face my sister. "Nahla, this is Aurora Maclay." Then I looked down at Aurora, who turned her head to study my lips. "My sister Nahla. The one I warned you about," I added for Nahla's sake.

Aurora turned back to Nahla. "It's very nice to meet you."

Nahla's eyes widened in surprise at Aurora's voice, and my damn chest acted up again at the sound of her words. She was going to talk to all of them. Not just my mother. She was using her voice to make them feel at ease. They had no idea how important this was, but I did.

"You're way too pretty for my brother," Nahla said as if she were talking to anyone.

Aurora smiled softly. "Thank you, but I don't agree." She turned those green eyes to me, and the softness in them was almost more than I could take. I was battling grabbing her and hauling her off like a possessive idiot so I could have her to myself. "Ryker is the most beautiful guy I've ever met." She'd never said those words to me before.

When she turned back to watch Nahla and see her response, I was still studying her. Unable to take my eyes off her. Not giving two shits my little sister was seeing me like this. Completely owned by a girl.

Nahla's eyebrows were both up as high as they could go, and she shook her head. "I'm gonna have to disagree with you on that one. I've seen your brother," she told Aurora.

That got a laugh from her, and just hearing it had my hand tightening on her waist. I'd never heard her laugh that loudly. I wanted more of it.

"I have drinks and cookies," my mother announced as she walked back into the room.

"We have Coke and cookies?" Nahla asked. "Since when? I was looking for a snack earlier."

"The Cherry Coke is for Aurora. Ryker had it in the fridge for her visit. Hidden from you. The cookies I bought at the bakery today. You can go fix yourself some milk" was Mom's response.

I hadn't been watching Aurora to see if she was getting any of this, but when she said, "She can have the Coke," I knew she had caught most of it.

Mom looked at me then. I had bought a liter of it, so I nodded at Nahla. "Go get you some."

She beamed happily and ran toward the kitchen.

Aurora's hand touched mine then. The one still on her waist. It wasn't to get me to let go but more of a pleased touch. She wanted me to know she liked how I treated my sister. The way Aurora used body language and touch to communicate made me feel like we had our own private way of talking. I liked it. I was getting better at noticing it and understanding it.

I wrapped two of my fingers around hers and held

them there for a moment before letting her go so we could sit on the sofa.

"We have chocolate chip cookies and sugar cookies," Mom told her.

"Thank you. I'm starving. My stepmother made dinner, and she's into healthy organic food. It was terrible." She spoke slowly, and I wondered how difficult it was to say that much without being able to hear her own voice. She spoke softly, but it was clear.

My mom laughed. "What did she cook?" she asked.

Aurora scrunched her perfect freckle-covered nose and replied, "Tofu."

"That sounds worse than the things you try to cook," my dad said to my mother as he walked into the room with his evening cup of coffee. I hadn't been sure where he was or if he was coming, but seeing him made me a little nervous. I didn't want him to make Aurora uncomfortable after she'd done so much to ease everyone else.

"I'm Anthony Lee," he said, walking over to Aurora with his hand held out. She slipped hers in his and shook it. "Glad you're here," he finished.

"It's nice to meet you," she said a little more cautiously than she had with my mom and sister.

Dad reached down and took a sugar cookie before taking the seat across from us. "How are you liking

Lawton?" Dad asked her before taking a bite.

She glanced at me and grinned before turning back to him. "A lot more than I thought I would."

My mom chuckled.

Dad pointed his half-eaten cookie at me. "Surely not because of this guy," he teased. His crooked grin said he liked her.

She shrugged her shoulders. "He might have a little to do with it."

"I won't judge you on your taste in guys," he said with a shake of his head.

Aurora smiled, then blushed. The pink was impossible to hide against her pale skin. I had the urge to grab her and take off with her again.

I nudged her arm, and she turned her attention to my mouth. "Eat a cookie. You're hungry," I told her. She was holding an uneaten chocolate chip cookie in her hand, but because she had to watch everyone to know if they were speaking to her, she hadn't taken a bite. It made me exhausted for her.

She gave me a soft smile before doing as I said.

"I like her," Nahla announced as she walked back into the room. I was glad Aurora hadn't seen her enter and seen my sister announce something like that. As if we had been waiting for her approval.

My mother nodded her head in agreement. "I understand now" was all she said.

Aurora finished her cookie, and I slipped my hand in hers. "Can we go to the den now? Or do y'all want to tell her why she shouldn't like me some more?" I made sure Aurora could see my mouth when I spoke.

"Yes, of course. Take the cookies, though. She's hungry," Mom said.

"Wait! Let me get one first!" Nahla called out, running over to grab two cookies. One of each.

I stood and took Aurora's empty hand as she reached to take the Cherry Coke with her other. I grabbed the plate of cookies that were left. "Thanks," I said to all of them.

Aurora simply smiled at them all, and I led her from the room before anyone could try and talk to her again. It was more work for her, and she'd been amazing. That was enough for tonight.

When we walked into the den, I set the cookies down on the first piece of furniture we came to, then took her Coke and set it down beside them before pulling her against me and kissing her. She let out a little surprised sound, then eased against me. Her body fitting me perfectly. This week had been the best one of my life. All because of her.

I Was Becoming a Rebel

CHAPTER 28

AURORA

The tension in my body was gone just that quickly. Being in Ryker's arms and the warmth of his body made everything okay . . . no, it made everything perfect. I'd been working so hard to make his family feel comfortable with me and like me that I hadn't realized how tense I was. But his magical mouth made it all better. When he pulled back only a few inches, his warm breath smelled like cookies. I leaned in and placed one more peck on his lips. I loved those lips.

He had been holding me to him, which made having to stand on my tiptoes easier. He held most of my weight and was basically picking me up. With reluctance, he let me back down slowly. I saw his eyes then, and there was

something different in them. A depth in his expression. I
had seen his cocky gleam and his pleased twinkle, but this
was new. It was neither. It was . . . more. It was important.
I could feel all those things.

I reached up and touched his cheek then. Silently we
stood like that staring at each other. No words were needed.

"You used your voice," he said.

I nodded.

"You didn't have to, and I understand how much it
meant that you did."

They had all seemed very happy to hear me speak.
No one had turned away from me or given any look that
showed it had bothered them. It had been a leap for me, but
I was thankful I'd done it.

"I wanted them to like me. I didn't think writing things
down would make it an easy meeting." Having to write to
communicate with people who weren't used to that never
went smoothly. With Ryker's family, I wasn't going to
make that mistake.

He took my hand again and lifted the corner of his
mouth in a half smile. "I was only concerned with you liking them."

He led me over to the sofa, then motioned for me to
sit down before going back to get the cookies and my
Coke he'd left on the table. I wasn't as hungry now that

we were alone. I just wanted to be with him. Enjoying the moment.

For the next hour we sat there close, holding hands, watching *The Walking Dead* on Netflix, and talking very little. It wasn't needed.

Hunter was making a habit out of being in my room when I got back from being with Ryker. This time I mentally prepared myself before opening the door, and I had been right to. Because there he sat on the end of my bed. His phone in his hand horizontally as if he were playing a game on it. More than likely he was playing *Fortnite*.

"What?" I asked him, using my voice. I'd done that a lot today. It was becoming natural. Easy. Something I didn't think about. I liked this new me.

"Nothing," he said with an annoyed glare in my direction. "I was staying in here in case Dad or Ella came to look for you."

I raised my eyebrow. "And what were you going to tell them if they did?" I signed this, not wanting them to hear me if they were in their room.

He shrugged. "I have no idea. I thought up a few excuses, but none sounded legit. So . . ." He held up his phone. "I decided to play."

Rolling my eyes, I walked past him and tossed my purse

on the nightstand. His being in here would have gotten him in trouble, because he would have obviously known I was gone. I turned back to him and signed, "Night before the big game, you should be in bed."

He smirked, not in a humored way either. "Ryker isn't in bed yet."

"He will be soon. Go," I replied.

Hunter pressed a few more buttons on his phone, then slipped it into his pocket. "Fine. I'm gone." He started for the door and paused, stood there a minute as if trying to decide what he was going to say, then turned back to me.

"Where did he take you?" he signed.

I knew he wanted to ask *What did you do?*

Tonight with Dad he had handled things well. The pressure was on him, and it was my fault in a way. Although my Dad's issues couldn't exactly be blamed on me. I did feel bad for Hunter.

"To his house. I met his parents and his sister. They gave me cookies and Cherry Coke."

Hunter cocked his head to the side and asked, "Really?"

I nodded.

"How did you talk to them?" He asked the obvious. I knew Ryker hadn't thought that through when he took me to meet them, but Hunter had lived his entire life with my deafness. It was his first thought with me. Which made me realize it hadn't been with Ryker. He didn't look at me and see just a deaf girl. I was smiling again.

"I used my voice," I said with confidence I honestly felt.

The shock on his face was unmistakable. "Really?" he asked in awe.

I nodded. "Really," I replied with my voice.

His smile was one that was unsure but proud. This thing with Ryker had him torn between concern for me and wanting me to be happy. We understood each other. We always had.

"Good night," he said with a small nod, then turned and walked out of the room. No more questions. How could he keep being negative after that information? He couldn't, and he was smart enough to let it go and get some sleep.

After all, tomorrow was a big day for him, Ryker, and the team. It was holding up my life and affecting my choices. That's how important it was. I sat down on my bed, thinking about how something like football could hold that much importance. I had forgotten what the world of football was like since Hunter and my dad had moved. It had been a big thing in our house from the time Hunter was four years old. Dad put a football in his hand and spent hours with him outside throwing it back and forth.

Now, after all these years and all this work, the time had come for it to mean something. Just like when we were kids and football came before anything I wanted to do, it was coming before what I wanted again. I'd learned to accept it at a young age. I wondered how many girls would do this.

I need to take off my clothes and get ready for bed. I thought about taking a shower, but I could smell Ryker's cologne on me from sitting so close, touching, and, of course, kissing. I decided I might just sleep in my shirt.

Slipping my bra off and tossing it in the laundry basket, I couldn't remember a time I had gone to bed dirty. I was becoming a rebel. That thought made me laugh.

Ready to Make History?

CHAPTER 29

RYKER

It was like electricity in the air, when it was game day. Today, however, it was more intense. Everyone could feel it. The energy rippled through the entire student body. Seeing Aurora was a struggle, though, because I was already missing the first half of the game, so being late to a class was pushing things. I couldn't give any teacher a reason to get me in trouble.

By noon, when the team had lunch separately from everyone else then loaded the buses to head to North Bank, which was a two-hour drive, I had only seen her twice and very briefly. I glanced around as we were sent from the gym, where they had fed us, to the waiting buses they'd leased for the trip. I didn't see her in the crowded hallway to our left. It wasn't time for her to be at this side of the hall, but I had hoped maybe she'd come see me before I left.

"She doesn't know the drill on game days like this," Hunter Maclay said as he walked up to my right side.

I glanced over at him. He had the same intense expression he wore every game day and on the field. No emotion. Just concentration. As if he were replaying every play in his head and preparing for anything that could be thrown our way by the opposing defense.

He cut his eyes at me. "You were looking in the crowd. Searching, more like it. I figured it was Aurora you were looking for. At least it better be after all this shit." He looked straight ahead again but kept in step beside me.

"Didn't see her much today. I should have told her we'd be going out at this time," I said honestly. Because he needed to know that she was exactly who I was looking for. No one else was in my thoughts.

"Best you didn't. Need your head clear" was his automatic response. This dude had serious issues. He put way too much importance on the game. Sure, I needed it to pay for my college too, but Jesus, he was a fucking drill sergeant.

"Seeing a girl before I play has never hurt my performance

before," I replied, wondering if this was something his dad had put in his head.

He didn't flinch. "You told me you've never felt like this about another girl. I'd think that might be different."

I had no response to that. Because he had a point, possibly. This was a first for me. But I didn't want to think not seeing Aurora would help me be more focused. "I think it'll make me think about her more. Wonder if she understands where I went and didn't get to say good-bye." *There, Hunter. How's that for honesty?*

We arrived at the line of players loading the bus and handing off their bags to the people putting them under the bus. He stopped then and turned toward me. "My sister understands football and its importance more than any other girl you've met. She knows. She understands."

She had grown up with Hunter and their father, who seemed to think football was above all else. It didn't mean it was above all else for me. I wasn't going to say that to him, though. He thought this was normal behavior.

"Ready to make history?" Nash asked as he slapped my shoulder and stepped in front of me to get on the bus. He was grinning like an idiot as he did it.

"Ask Hunter—I only get the last half," I reminded him.

Nash didn't say anything, but I could tell the reason why annoyed him. He wasn't going to get over my losing it on Asa anytime soon. Even though Asa and I were good. Nash would love to be out on that field again. I wouldn't let the fact he couldn't play anymore make me feel guilty for messing up my chance at playing the entire game.

What was done was done.

"No one has to question Hunter. We all know he's ready" was Nash's response; then he went inside to find a seat.

I handed my bag off to one of the men loading the bus, then followed Nash inside. I wasn't sitting by his ass, though. I wanted silence. Most of us did. My Beats were in my backpack I still had on my back. My ritual pregame playlist was on my phone, and I planned on sitting in a window seat and listening to it with my eyes closed. Blocking out the rest of the bullshit.

Hunter was behind me, and I knew he would do the same, but I doubted he'd choose to take a seat beside me. We were on good terms with my dating Aurora, but having to hide that from his dad made it tense between us. Like we were having to hide a major secret that could unravel both our lives. Which was fucking ridiculous.

Tonight I wanted us to win. We all did. Many of the guys on this bus would go to college on tonight's performance. It was vitally important to us all. My parents could afford to send me to college, but they'd have to get some financial aid, and I'd need a student loan or two. They didn't want that and neither did I, but we could do it. However, there were guys who would have to get jobs here in Lawton and go to the local junior college, if they even got to do that. There would be many who became coal miners like their fathers. We all wanted more.

I sat down on a seat near the middle and got comfortable. The back of the bus tended to get rowdy for the first part of the trip. We all handled the pregame differently. The younger boys were high on their adrenaline. I was one of them once. They didn't have the weight of college on them yet. They wouldn't be playing much either. The middle of the bus was the starters, the juniors and seniors who knew this was important. More than walking around with our chests puffed out because we won. We needed this. For the seniors, this could be the last time we played with our team. The guys we'd grown up on the field with. Possibly the last time we played at all.

The front of the bus was the coaches. They'd talk strategy, work through issues, and rethink everything they'd already talked about. Nash was up there with them. He should be here beside me, with his headphones on, listening to music and focusing on making sure this game put us on the field at an SEC school next year. I had battled with that already and come to terms with it. Nash wouldn't play again. He had found his peace as well. But facing this tonight and looking up at the back of his head while he discussed the defense with Coach Rich, I missed what could have been.

My chest ached for a moment when I thought about how he was feeling right now. I knew him well. We'd grown up like brothers. This was important to him because of me. He couldn't do this, but he wanted it for me. He wanted me to get to do what we had always planned on. The start of the school year he had struggled. Hard. He'd messed up, and I wasn't sure he'd be sitting there where he was right now if it wasn't for Tallulah. She'd saved him when no one else could.

That brought my thoughts back to Aurora, and for a moment I had a slight fear I had been looking for someone to save me. From what, I didn't know. But I had wanted her the moment I saw her, and that wasn't normal. Not for anyone. Unless it was one of those dumbass shows my sister watched on television in the afternoons. I closed my eyes and blocked out everything around me, the music on my playlist pumping in my ears.

Aurora would still be here next year when I left. She'd have one more year of high school. She could be hundreds of miles away from me. I'd barely see her. Shit. The ache in my chest thinking about Nash was now so damn tight at the idea of not seeing Aurora that I had to inhale deeply, hoping to ease it. This was not something I could let affect me. Especially tonight.

I felt someone take the seat beside me, but I didn't open my eyes to see who it was. I didn't care as long as they left me the hell alone. I had to get myself together mentally. Aurora was new; she was sweet; she made me happy. That was all I needed to think about. I didn't have to worry about the future. It was months away.

In a few hours, however, I would have something to worry about. Something that was important to the here and now. Nash was sitting up front, unable to play the game we both loved. He had played his last game already and at the time had no idea. I knew tonight could be my last high school game. It was knowledge that brought me back around to my main focus right now.

Football.

Football in Alabama
Was a Big Deal

CHAPTER 30

AURORA

My dad seemed pleased that I was riding to the game with Tallulah. I was surprised. I thought it might be a bit of a fight. The drive to North Bank was a long one. I hadn't known that when she'd asked me if I wanted to go with her to the game. However, Dad had surprised me and said sure. Dad rarely spent much time talking to me. Even when I was younger, it was Hunter he focused on. I got a few moments of attention, but we didn't have a relationship like I knew other girls had with their fathers. I had seen it at my old school. Fathers who came to our different events. Mine came occasionally and left shortly after arriving. He didn't ask me about anything. Even the play I had been

Jane in, *Pride and Prejudice*. Hunter had football practice that night, so he hadn't shown up. No explanation.

Getting a simple *sure* out of him was surprising, but then I figured if he'd said no, it would have caused him to need to think about it, and he was focused on the game. As if he were about to play in it.

He had left earlier, following the buses. My riding with Tallulah meant Ella didn't have to go, and she really didn't want to drive that far to watch football. Dad didn't say that; he said, "I'm glad you're making friends with good people." I'm sure he meant that too, but he was also thinking, *Now Ella won't complain and moan about having to come to this game.*

School let out at one thirty, once the buses carrying the players, cheerleaders, and band members were gone. The moment all three buses had cleared the parking lot, the announcement came over the PA along with a lot of "Go Lions!" and cheering. Tallulah was going to pick me up at three thirty, so we both had time to go home, shower off school, and get ready. She mentioned getting dinner somewhere in North Bank, since we would have two hours before the game started. It all depended on the traffic in town.

Football in Alabama was a big deal. I was learning that more and more. The stores in town had changed their signs to GO LIONS! and school colors were flying everywhere.

People even had signs in their yards with players' last names and numbers on them. If you ever wondered where a player in Lawton lived, you could ride around and read the signs. Sure, some of them had their names in a few yards, but it was a family member's house if it wasn't their own. This was all a new experience. Hunter was used to it. Me, not so much.

I stood at my bedroom window looking down at the new sign that was triple the size of the one we'd had when I arrived last week. It had a large MACLAY on it with #9 underneath it. Of course it boldly stated he was the QB on there as well. I had fought the urge to roll my eyes when Ella had pulled into the driveway this afternoon and I'd seen the new signage decorating our yard. It was a bit much, and I doubted Hunter was real thrilled. He didn't care about the bragging. He just wanted to win.

If they lost, would Dad take it down? Shrugging off that pointless thought, I went to check myself in the mirror one last time before going downstairs to wait on Tallulah. It was going to get down to the forties tonight. Fall was finally arriving in Alabama. It took a while, that was for sure. I'd decided on a pair of fitted dark-wash jeans with no holes and a Lawton-blue sweater I already owned before moving here; it was lower cut than I normally wore and cropped at the waist. Mom had bought it for me last year,

and I'd never worn it. Tonight, though, it seemed appropri-
ate. I'd kept my hair down, but I had a ponytail holder on
my wrist in case the wind picked up and the curls wouldn't
stay out of my face. My shoes I had changed about three
times. Finally deciding on my black Doc Martens boots.
They looked good with the outfit, and my feet would stay
warm. Grabbing my black puffy North Face coat, I decided
I might need gloves as well. Once I had all of it together, I
headed downstairs to the living room.

Ella was sitting in the recliner, watching someone reno-
vate a house on television and drinking a hot tea. She smiled
up at me and spoke slowly. Almost so slowly it was hard to
read her lips. I wondered if she was yelling again.

"You look beautiful," she said with sincerity, even if she
looked weird opening her mouth so wide.

Thank you, I said silently.

"Do you need money?" she asked. She felt awkward
talking to me. I could tell. We really needed to work on
my conversing with her. This was just too strange. Maybe
I could start using my voice. I did it with Ryker's family.
This was my stepmother, and I was being difficult by holding back on her.

"Dad gave me some this morning," I said with my voice
this time.

Her eyes widened at the sound, and I waited as she sat

there in surprise. Then she did the unexpected and set her cup down, jumped out of her seat, and grabbed me in a hug. I wasn't a big hugger, probably because my parents didn't hug much or at all. I stood there a moment before hugging her back with my one arm that wasn't full of outerwear. It was brief, and I dropped my hands quickly. Not sure I wanted to move to the hugging stage with her.

She stepped back, and I saw tears on her cheeks as she grinned too brightly and wiped at her face. "I'm sorry," she said as she dried her eyes. "I didn't mean to get emotional. But thank you. For that." She said this all normally. No big, slow words. I felt guilty now for not doing it before. My own insecurities had made her feel left out or something.

"It's okay," I said, and saw her face light up even more. She was young, she cooked terrible food, and she was a little annoying, but I saw why Dad loved her. She wasn't bad. She was kind. Just quirky, different from what I knew. Who was I to judge someone being different? After I had thoroughly chastised myself for treating her poorly and not even realizing it, I smiled at her. "Thanks for asking if I needed money."

She continued that one-hundred-watt beam of hers while I saw Tallulah's car turn into the driveway. I'd had enough emotional bonding with my stepmother. I was more than relieved to see Tallulah. "My ride is here. Enjoy your night," I told her.

"You too!" she said cheerily, and I could see more tears well up in her eyes. I got the heck out of there before the crying started up again.

Closing the door behind me, I checked to make sure my purse was on my shoulder and my phone in my pocket before walking out to Tallulah's car. I opened the front driver's-side door and tossed my coat and gloves into the backseat, then sat down.

Tallulah signed and said, "You don't have a scarf. I have two Lawton-colored ones my mother made in the back if you want to use one."

I nodded and replied, "Thank you," using my voice. "All I had Lawton-colored was this sweater."

She raised her eyebrows. "I'm jealous of that sweater. It's super cute."

"Thanks," I replied.

"You have everything you need?" she asked.

"Yes. I'm ready," I assured her.

She nodded and then began backing out of the driveway.

"That sign is a bit much," I said, then glanced over at her.

The corner of her mouth lifted. "Nash said the Booster Club made them."

I didn't say any more, because she had to watch the road

to drive. She wouldn't be able to look at me and respond so I could understand. But hearing that the Booster Club had supplied the sign made more sense. I leaned back in my seat and reached for my phone in my pocket so it wasn't poking me in the butt. Glancing down at it, I wondered if I should text Ryker, or if that was a distraction for him. I knew Hunter was one-track minded on game day. Ryker was already sitting out the first half. After studying his last text to me, I decided that was meant as a "last text until the game was over," and I put my phone back in my lap. Football came first. That much I knew.

What if It Wasn't My Dream?
CHAPTER 31

RYKER

Richards had come to play ball. That was for damn sure. No wonder the guy was the number one scouted quarterback in Alabama this year. He was North Bank's lethal weapon, and when he graduated, they weren't going to be nearly as strong. I glanced up at the scoreboard, already knowing what it said. They were ahead by a touchdown. It could be worse. If it hadn't been for our defense, they'd have two more scores on that board. Hunter was playing his best game, though. I'd give him that. We had hung in there and scored twice because he could put that ball in in the hand of a receiver you didn't even realize was open. McNair had missed two passes he shouldn't have, though. If I had been on the field, I knew we'd be ahead. Maclay had made it happen even with McNair's mess-ups. He'd be the number one scouted QB next year. Especially after this game.

"You ready?" Nash asked me.

I was. I had been all the first half. Now it was finally time for the offense to take the field for the first time in the second half, and my adrenaline was pumping in my veins. I'd stayed focused. The few times I'd allowed Aurora to creep into my thoughts, I'd fought the urge to look back into the stands for her. I knew she was here. That's all that mattered. I had to win this game. Then I'd celebrate with her beside me.

"Yes," I said as I slipped my helmet on.

"Give 'em hell," he called out as I ran onto the field. The smell of the grass, the sounds of the bands and yells coming from the stands, the intensity of everyone around me. I loved this feeling. Having to watch it and not participate had been hard. It reminded me how Nash must feel, and I knew I was out here for him, too.

My eyes locked with Maclay's, and he gave me a look I knew. This was me. I had to get open. I blinked at him twice to let him know I was ready, then took my place on the line.

It all went like a fucking dance. One we had memorized. The team had been working with McNair and Judson all night. I knew they'd studied me in previous games, just as we had their key players, but being on the field with the sudden change was still enough to mess with their heads.

I was down right field, and the ball was in my hands before they knew what was happening. Then there was my speed. Something else McNair lacked. He could catch the ball, but he couldn't outrun the defense.

I could and I did.

The roar that erupted as my foot hit the grass just over the end zone was familiar and only made the fire in us all burn brighter.

I was engulfed by the guys closest to me. "Fuck yeah!" "That's Lawton ball!" and other things were being yelled as they celebrated, and we headed to the sidelines, where the rest of the team was jumping and cheering.

Nash was there to greet me, and he put both his hands on my shoulders. "That's how a Lee does it," he said, grinning.

I winked at him, and he laughed. Then I turned to see Maclay watching us. He gave me a nod. I nodded back. We'd tied the game, and we both knew we could win this.

When the moment of the last few seconds on the clock finally came, the crowd behind us began chanting "Lawton" over and over. We had scored two more times, and North Bank had only scored once. Our defense was strong enough to fight back, and no matter how good Richards was, he didn't have anyone fast enough to outrun us.

The seconds ticked down as Richards sent a beautiful pass to his receiver, and when he caught it, there was silence for only a moment. Because a Lion took down the receiver before he even got to take one step. Game over. Lawton won.

I didn't join the others yelling. I turned then and looked up into the crowd of blue. Shakers and cowbells were everywhere, as was the excitement. We'd be going to State. I scanned them all, thinking it was going to be impossible to find her in all this, and just as I started to give up, I saw her step out onto the path of stairs to the far right. The red hair was hard to miss. She paused, as if she realized I was looking for her, and then she waved.

I held up my hand and waved back.

Neither of us thinking about who was watching. Not caring at the moment. All I could think about was I'd get to celebrate with her tonight at the field. It would be late, but even if we got home at midnight, everyone would head to the field. It was tradition. I wanted to run out of this fence and up there to meet her. Grab her and kiss her right here in front of them all. Smell her and feel her against me. But I couldn't. She wouldn't be able to run out on the field to congratulate me either. Her dad was out here. He would see it. I had no reason to stand out here and wait for someone. There was no one else I wanted to see.

"You did it, Son," my dad's voice said, interrupting my

thoughts. I turned to see him beside me. His gaze went to where mine had been. "Even with the new distraction in your life. You stayed focused. You'll have to be ready to make your decision on where you want to play. Because after that performance, you'll get more than one offer."

"Thanks" was all I said, not liking the way he had called Aurora my new distraction, but also not wanting to argue with him after that game. I wanted to ride the high of the moment. I noticed Maclay wasn't celebrating as hard as the others either. He was smiling as big as I'd ever seen him, but he was calmer. Still focused. His dad was beside him, and he seemed more than pleased, but he was talking to Hunter. As if going over the game with him. That shit had to be annoying.

Hunter's dad's head turned at that moment, and his eyes locked with mine. He held that, and I didn't look away. He was sizing me up. Trying to figure something out, and I knew exactly what that something was. My interest in his daughter. I nodded respectfully, then headed for the field house to get showered and changed for the ride back on the bus.

"He still doesn't know," my dad said as he walked beside me.

I didn't have to ask him what or who he was talking about. "No."

Dad didn't respond right away. Then he said, "I think he has an idea."

"Me too," I agreed.

"You got your uncle's speed!" Nash's father said as he stepped in front of us. Then he hugged me hard and slapped my back. "Your daddy was too damn slow," he added with a smirk in his brother's direction.

Dad rolled his eyes. "Fuck that," he said, and my uncle laughed loudly.

"No one has ever been able to stop a Lee," my uncle added. "Even your slow-ass father."

Both my dad and uncle had played college ball. Neither had made it to the NFL, for different reasons. Ones they didn't talk about, even if we already knew the truth. This town was small. Hard to keep secrets. It was my uncle's reason that scared my dad about me. Because if he hadn't fallen in love with my aunt his senior year, my uncle wouldn't have kept coming back to Lawton and, in the end, chosen this life over the one he could have lived.

I didn't think his life was a bad one, and my dad wanting me to have something he thought was more didn't seem fair. What if I didn't want to live the life he wished he'd had? What if it wasn't my dream? What if I messed it all up, and when the hell did life decisions get so hard?

CHAPTER 32

AURORA

I watched him until he disappeared into the field house. Tallulah and I made our way to the field just as Nash was coming toward her. He had a slight limp, but it was not very noticeable unless he was moving fast. Like he was now. She smiled and hugged him tightly, then he kissed her firmly on the mouth. I looked away to give them privacy, although they were in a crowd of people. I found my dad walking back this way from the field house. His gaze landed on me, and he headed in my direction.

The excitement on every face around me was fun to watch. I had never been nervous watching a football game until tonight. When Ryker stepped out onto the field, I'd been anxious. Wanting him to do good, and he'd done more than that. He and Hunter had played together perfectly. I had no idea Ryker was so fast, either, until I'd seen him leave the others so far behind they had no hope of catching up. Tallulah had signed to me after his touchdown that he was known for his speed.

I could understand why.

Now, the game was won, and I could face telling my dad about Ryker. After the way Ryker and Hunter had been so unstoppable together, I didn't think he'd be negative about it. I wanted to have the freedom to rush onto the field and kiss Ryker.

When Dad reached me, he stopped and smiled at Tallulah and Nash. "Hello, great game."

Both of them agreed, and then he turned back to me. "Does Tallulah want you to ride home with her, or is Nash going to ride back with her?" Dad asked me in sign as well as speaking.

I glanced at her and realized I hadn't thought of this. I hoped I didn't have to ride home with Dad, but then it wouldn't be fair to be a bother to Tallulah.

"We are going to the field to celebrate with everyone and would love for Aurora to go with us," Tallulah replied, also signing as she spoke.

Dad frowned, and I waited. Hunter would be going to

the field. There was no question about that. His pause in my going had to do with Ryker. It wasn't fair that he was reacting this way.

"Okay, but you need to ride home from the field with Hunter. It's too late for a field party, but I will allow you both to go for an hour once we get back to Lawton." He signed this and again said the words for the others.

I nodded, relieved that I was getting to go without a fight. "Yes, sir," I signed in response. He started to leave, then paused and looked at me one more time. As if he could read my mind if he looked closely enough. I met his gaze and held it. It almost felt as if I were challenging him. Asking him to say something. Tell me I couldn't see Ryker when he didn't know that I was.

Finally he turned and walked back toward where the buses had pulled up and players were slowly coming from the field house with their bags and loading up. Turning to Tallulah, I wondered if she'd picked up on any of that. Or worse, if Nash had. I signed thank you to her and then looked at Nash and smiled. He seemed concerned, but he returned the smile. He had definitely figured out some of it.

I wanted to explain it, but I didn't understand it either. How could I explain something that made no sense to me? Several people stopped to say something to Nash about the game. He was genuinely happy for the team, even though he no longer was able to play. Tallulah's hand was holding on to his, and I knew it was a silent form of support. Their body language said a lot about them. They'd both graduate this May, and they could go to the same college. I envied them what they had.

"There's Ryker," Tallulah said, and pointed behind me. That was enough to make me forget everything else. Spinning around, I found him instantly, and the way his eyes lit up when they met mine made it all okay. No matter what happened with my dad, it was going to be okay. I was sure of it.

I began making my way toward him, and we met in the middle of the crowd still celebrating on the field. His hair was freshly washed, and he was wearing a Lawton Lions Football hoodie with a pair of sweats that matched. He smelled good. I stared up at him in awe at how he could play a game that intense and be so beautiful minutes afterward. He didn't even appear exhausted.

"Are you riding back with Tallulah?" he asked, his eye locked on mine as he kept a bit of a distance. Not touching me. Just close enough to hear me if I spoke, and so I could see his lips.

"Yes," I told him.

"Good, then I am too," he said with a soft grin that seemed a touch wicked. Like he was doing something wrong and going to get away with it.

I hadn't thought about him riding back with us. Never crossed my mind. The excitement of riding with him in the backseat of Tallulah's car, however, was immediate. "Okay." I said the word, wondering if my voice sounded as giddy as I felt.

He glanced back over his shoulder, scanning the crowd, and I wondered who he was looking for, but then his eyes came back to me. "Where's your dad?"

"He left."

"Thank God" was his response, and I laughed, which only made his grin bigger.

He lifted his gaze then to look over my shoulder. He was listening to someone, but I didn't turn to see who. I watched his mouth instead. Finally he said, "It's fine. I'll make sure no one sees me get in the back. I'm not riding back on the damn bus when she's in the car with y'all." I wanted to kiss him. Seeing his scowl as he spoke to who I could guess was Nash, because he'd never look at Tallulah like he was annoyed. "I got this," he said again to Nash; then his gaze dropped back to mine. I wanted him with me too, but I didn't want him to be in any more trouble with the coach.

"Are you supposed to ride back on the bus?" I asked him.

He shook his head. "No, they let us ride back with

family or friends. We just have to text Coach to let him know we left with someone else and who."

I felt better. If Nash was just worried about my dad, then that was not an issue. He was gone. He'd never know.

"I'm going to go ahead and get my bag in the back of Tallulah's car, and I'll meet y'all there," he told me, then winked before walking away with Nash beside him. I watched him go for a few seconds, wondering what this feeling was that had grown so incredibly strong so fast. Then I turned back to Tallulah. She raised her eyebrows at me with an amused gleam in her eyes. "He's so different with you," she signed, looking a bit amazed. "I've never seen him like this, and I've known him since we were kids. He never knew I existed until this year, but I saw him. Mostly because I was always watching Nash, and they were together."

That was odd. Why hadn't Ryker known she existed until this year? "How did he not know you? The school isn't that big."

She looked as if she didn't want to say more. Or there was something she wasn't sure I should know. That made me want to know everything, of course.

"I was overweight until this summer. I lost weight. It was because . . ." She stopped a moment, and I wondered if she was struggling to finish or wasn't sure of the sign for the next thing she needed to say. Then she continued, "Someone said something that hurt me. I lost weight for the wrong reasons. But losing weight made others notice me."

She didn't say more. She dropped her hands and shrugged as if that was it. I knew there was more, but I let it go. I didn't want to push her. She motioned her head in the direction of the parking lot. "Let's go." She said the words.

I gave a quick nod, and we walked in the direction the guys had gone. I couldn't help but try and picture Tallulah overweight. It was impossible. She seemed confident and carried herself in a way that said she had never worried about her appearance or anything else. The kindness in her that I had noticed the very first day I met her made sense now. The idea of someone saying something hurtful to her made me angry. It was silly of course, since she'd made her peace with it and moved on, but it still bothered me. I knew more than anyone it was what was inside that counted. I'd seen evil in the eyes of those who were gorgeous on the outside. Like the girl my brother was currently dating.

The parking lot was full of people getting in their cars, and the only light came from the headlights as they pulled away. It felt safe in the darkness, and when we reached Tallulah's car, there were no lights on inside or out. She went to the front passenger seat, and I stopped at the door beside her. We looked at each other, then both pulled open our doors and climbed inside. It was dark, but I could see Ryker waiting on me in the backseat. The warmth from his body felt good after the coldness outside. I shivered, but I wasn't sure if it was the excitement of being back here with him or the sudden warmth reminding me of the low temperature outside.

He reached over and pulled me against his side. Once he had me in the middle of the backseat, he began to buckle the middle lap belt over me. It was too dark for us to speak, but I liked the darkness and being close to him. I inhaled and enjoyed the clean smell of his soap and the hint of cologne I had smelled earlier. My heart was beating faster than normal, but when he put his arm behind me, I eased back and laid my head on his chest.

I didn't have to worry about reading lips or following conversation. I could feel if he spoke by the vibration in his chest. He wasn't talking to Nash and Tallulah. I had no idea if they were talking, but I didn't care. It was like we were alone back here in our own little world. I wanted to stay this way forever.

Ryker began to play with my hair, and I sighed with pleasure. It felt amazing. His left hand found mine, and instead of linking my hand with his, I began to softly caress it. I felt his body tremble slightly when I began, and I loved that he couldn't see my face as I smiled. Pleased that I had affected him this way.

There was a slight vibration in his chest. He'd said something. It sounded like one word. I knew it wasn't to me, so I didn't lift my head to be nosy. Nash was probably talking to him. It was several minutes; then he said something else. Not much. A couple of words at best. His hand that had been playing with my hair found my ear and began softly running a fingertip to trace it. I closed my eyes again and slowly relaxed.

CHAPTER 33

RYKER

I could tell the moment her breathing slowed and her hand, which had been caressing mine, went still. She was asleep. I didn't stop touching her, though. Feeling her hair run through my fingers and having her curled up asleep on me was heaven. Hell, I didn't think heaven could get this good.

"Her dad knows something. I could tell by the way he was acting tonight," Nash said.

I was ready to deal with her dad and get it over with. "I'm going to handle that this week," I said.

"She can feel the vibration on your chest and knows you're talking. It's rude to talk about things concerning her with her right here in the car," Tallulah scolded us both.

"She's asleep," I said, agreeing with Tallulah. If she had been awake, I'd have made sure she knew what we were saying.

Earlier Nash had said something about me being quiet after a big win, and I'd just grunted in response. Then he'd said if he didn't know better, he'd think I was in love. I had replied, "Yeah."

That had silenced him. It had been a vague answer. Because if I was going to say that I loved Aurora, then it would be to her. Not to Nash. She hadn't lifted her head to see what I was saying, and I was glad.

I'd never told a girl I loved her before. Not counting my mom and sister. But that's completely different. This kind of love was new for me. It felt amazing and terrifying. Admitting to myself that I'd fallen in love for the first time in my life with a girl I had only known for five days was hard to do. I'd have laughed my ass off at any other guy in my position.

I hadn't even been sure I believed in love at this age until Aurora. I thought it was lust and the need to have someone close. It wasn't. I got that now.

Looking down at her, I moved her back as easy as I could onto my arm, so her face was tilted toward me and I could see her perfect, delicate features. The freckles on her face always got me in the chest. She'd taught me a lot this week. More than I'd ever learned in such a short time.

Love was finding your own happiness in witnessing someone else's. It was finding perfect peace in simply holding that person in your arms. Love was the sudden burst of joy from their smile. Wanting to know everything about someone from their dreams to their favorite food to their best memory as a child. It had nothing to do with lust. That was what surprised me the most.

I wasn't saying I didn't want to do things with her, because I did. My imagination went there often, and the kissing only made it get more out of hand. In time, I knew more would come when she was ready, and if that took forever I'd wait. That was love too, I realized.

She made a soft sound and moved closer to me, her hand found my chest, and she turned into me and placed it there almost directly over my heart. I reached up and covered her hand with my own. It was so small compared to mine.

"Tallulah, I'm sorry. I know I've said it before, but I need you to know I mean it. I hate myself for what I said about you. I hate knowing I hurt you. I don't ever want to be that guy again. I can't think of one thing about him that was likable." I wasn't sure why the sudden apology for something that had happened last May had come out of my mouth, but I needed to say it.

"You've been forgiven. But thank you. Besides, if you hadn't said it . . ." She paused, and I wondered how much of that moment she wanted to recap with Nash listening. It was hard on him, too, remembering that time in our life. "I wouldn't have . . . this."

I didn't say anything then, because that was a touchy subject between her and Nash. I pressed a kiss to Aurora's forehead instead, then leaned my head back and closed my eyes. Enjoying this more than tonight's victory.

"I'd have still gotten hurt, I'd have still been bitter and angry, and there isn't a soul who could have reached me but you. There isn't one who would have loved me enough to try," I heard Nash say.

I smiled in the darkness. I had to agree with him. He'd been hard to deal with after his accident, and it took someone who had loved him all his life the way Tallulah had, to put up with his crap and pull him out of it. Her weight had nothing to do with that, and she'd never been invisible to Nash. He'd been defending her since first grade.

A hand touched my cheek then, and my eyes snapped open. I lifted my head back up, and my eyes met Aurora's. This time she'd been watching me sleep, or so she thought. I'd been awake. The corners of her full lips curled up, and I bent my head as she lifted hers. The moment our lips met, my chest felt like it was so full it would explode.

She turned more and slid her hand that had been on my face into my hair as she opened her lips for me. I took complete advantage of the invitation and savored her sweet taste. My hands slid down to her waist, and I let my left one slowly move back up her side until it rested just under the cup of her breast. The sharp inhale of her breath reminded me to pause. Not to push for more.

Thankfully, she didn't pull away or break the kiss. She pressed her chest against mine; then, surprising me, her kiss became more needy. That simple move had my pulse racing, and I tried to ease her back some to calm myself a moment. Her small sound of distress at my subtle move had me pulling her closer again. I didn't like thinking she was upset, and, hell, if pressing her chest against me and kissing me more aggressively was what she wanted, I'd let her. I could handle it without moving too fast and forgetting myself.

Then her right leg came over mine as she twisted into me more, and it slid between my thighs, causing her to straddle my left leg. Her left hand slid up my chest, and I had to shift slightly, which set her directly on my thigh.

My hand that had been resting under her breast was now covering her breast, but not because I'd moved it there; her body shifting had placed it there before I realized what was happening. I stilled. My entire body froze, and I took very deep, long breaths as I waited to see what she was going to do. Our lips were barely an inch apart, and her panting breaths were mingled with mine. I stared into her eyes as she looked at me. Neither of us moving.

Her position on my leg and my hand completely covering her right breast stayed as they were, waiting. She had to guide this. It had to be her. I didn't think I could make smart decisions at the moment.

She took a deep breath then, and the rise and fall of her chest made my hand full of her breast move. I had to swallow hard. This was almost too much. I started to chant the word *innocent* over and over in my head when she reached down and placed her hand over mine, then moved it just slightly over herself. She inhaled sharply then, and her eyes fluttered a little at the touch, and I was so close to losing my mind I didn't know how much more I could handle.

Then she took my hand away, and I didn't have time to decide if I was disappointed or relieved when she continued to move it until it was underneath the short sweater she was wearing, and all I felt was warm, soft skin as she slid it up until I was once again covering her breast, but with only a thin, lacy bra as the barrier. The swell of her breast was under my fingertips. She removed her hand then and placed it on my chest. Her eyes never leaving mine.

Innocent. She was so damn innocent. She had no idea how this was affecting me. Any other girl I'd accuse of being a tease. But that was definitely not what this was, and

I wasn't about to call her out on the movement and try and get her naked in the backseat while my cousin and his girlfriend were in the front seat.

The darkness had given her a sense of privacy, I assumed, but I was very aware that, even though they had the radio on, they knew exactly what was going on back here. I just had to get enough willpower to stop it. Aurora moved against my thigh, and her eyes closed as she inhaled from the feeling. I knew then she was so lost in the way this felt she wasn't thinking about the others in the car, and she'd regret it later.

I also didn't like the idea of any other man hearing the sexy little sounds she had no idea she was making. Which made them even more irresistible, because they weren't sounds she was faking to turn me on. Hers were completely authentic.

I moved my hand to her waist and grabbed it to keep her from moving any more; then I lifted her and moved her to sit beside me, thinking all the while I needed a fucking gold medal for this. Anything I'd done that would have kept me out of heaven should now be erased. Once I had her sweet body off me, I pulled her tightly against me and pressed a kiss to her head, not trusting myself to kiss anywhere closer to her mouth.

She was very still, and I wanted to talk to her about

this. I didn't want her to think I wasn't attracted to her. I hoped she realized why I had moved her off me. When the lights from the town filled the darkness in the car, I noticed for the first time we were already back in Lawton. That had been the fastest two hours of my life. I wasn't ready to be back, but then again I wanted Aurora alone. Nash's eyes met mine in the rearview mirror, and I could see he was impressed with me. Just like I thought, he'd been aware of it all, even if he'd been driving.

I ran my hand over Aurora's right arm, needing to feel her skin and reassure her if she needed it. I wasn't sure just yet, and I was afraid to look at her, because if she looked hurt, I wasn't going to be able to wait until I got her alone to tell her why I had stopped. That was something I knew she didn't want talked about in front of anyone else.

For her sake, I kept my eyes on the road and waited, knowing we'd be to the field in a few minutes. I would make it all better, and if she wanted to try more, I was willing to let her. I was hers to do with what she wanted.

"Could you drive us back to the barn first," I asked Nash as he pulled onto the road leading to the field.

He shook his head, and I started to tell him to drive the damn car back to the barn and let us out when the words fell silent on my lips. I saw the SUV ahead blocking our path now. I'd have recognized it even if Aurora's father hadn't been standing outside it with his hands crossed over his chest and his feet apart in a stance full of fury and impatience.

"Oh God," Aurora said aloud as she sat up straight out of my arms and saw him there. He was already moving toward her side of the car before Nash brought it to a complete stop.

"Shit," Nash muttered. Then all hell broke loose.

CHAPTER 34

AURORA

It had all happened too fast. I was embarrassed by my reaction to Ryker and his gentle rejection, if that was even what it was. I'd been trying to figure out if I had made a huge mistake. If he'd back away from me for it. All of that had my head in chaos, so I hadn't been paying attention. But it all ended immediately, and those worries no longer mattered.

My father was here.

He was waiting on me. He knew . . . he knew I was with Ryker, and Hunter was correct. He wasn't okay with it. Before I could even prepare to stand my ground, the passenger-side door was jerked open by my dad. Ryker's hand tried to clasp mine as I moved away from him and toward the door. I pulled my hand free and got out of the car to face my father.

"Get in the truck now," he said, signing in what I would guess was a threatening tone as he spoke.

I shook my head no, and his eyes widened in surprise. "It wasn't a request," he signed this time without speaking. "It was an order."

I didn't move. He was furious, but so was I. "You said I could come to the field party," I signed back at him.

He pointed at the car behind me, then signed, "I didn't say you could ride in the backseat of a car with that boy."

"His name is Ryker. And we weren't alone. Tallulah and Nash were in the car too. I don't see what the problem is," I replied with sign only.

His eyes flared angrily. He didn't expect me to stand up to him. He thought I'd go meekly to his truck. Wrong. If he had an issue, I wanted to know what it was.

"If you are with a boy, I need to know. I'm your father."

"I need to tell you I am riding in a car with my friends? You knew that already."

My dad looked back toward the car, then signed, "Is he your friend? You were all pressed up against him in the backseat. Didn't look friendly to me."

"He is more than a friend. We are dating," I said with

sign only. Knowing there were others watching us. We had drawn attention to ourselves. I saw Dad's gaze move and knew Ryker must have gotten out of the car. He was glaring in that direction.

"I didn't approve of that." He said the words this time. His glare still behind me.

"And I didn't know I needed your approval," I replied with my voice.

That got his attention, and he turned his glare to me this time. "You live in my house; you obey my rules. This is breaking my rules."

"What is? Me dating someone without your permission?"

He pointed at his SUV again. "Get in the truck!" he said, but I read his lips clearly. Then he signed, "We will discuss this at home."

I had a decision to make. Refuse to leave or go home and deal with this. People were watching. If my dad did have an issue with Ryker's skin color, then I didn't want that said here. In front of him or anyone else. I turned back around and saw Ryker standing there, waiting; he looked so torn. Like he wanted to help me but didn't know what to say or if he should.

"I'll text you," I said to him, then walked past my dad and went to get in his vehicle.

I jerked open the passenger door on his SUV and started to climb inside when I realized Ryker had moved and was closer to my dad, talking. In the night I couldn't see him well enough from here to see his mouth or know what he was saying, but he threw his hands up in frustration as he said something. I gave my dad a quick glance to see that he was talking too, but his face was stern. Then he turned his back on Ryker and stalked to the SUV.

Ryker was standing there looking angry and helpless all at once. I lifted my hand to wave good-bye, then climbed inside, leaving him there. I hated this. I shouldn't be leaving. This was a big night for him. I wanted to celebrate with everyone else.

Dad was inside and pulling out of the woods within seconds. I hadn't seen Hunter anywhere. Why hadn't he tried to help? Where was he? Was he getting to stay at the field?

I stared out the window into the side mirror. Ryker stood watching us leave. Nash walked up beside him, but it was too dark and too far away. I had no idea what they were doing now. Then the SUV turned onto the main road, and the sight of Ryker was gone.

Closing my eyes, I laid my head back on the seat and fought against the tears. I wasn't going to cry in here with my father to witness. He was being unfair and cruel. My mother would have never reacted this way. But then if I had been with my mother, I'd never found out all I was missing. If I had known all this, I wouldn't have been so upset and angry with my mom when she decided to move to California with her boyfriend. At the time I was sure my life was going to change for the worse. I missed Hunter, but my dad I was never sure about. Things had been so very different than I imagined. If Mom hadn't sent me to live with my dad, I'd never have come to Lawton and met Ryker. Or Tallulah.

I didn't want to lose either of them. This week had been perfect. I'd fit in. It hadn't been a world of seclusion like I had prepared myself for. Forgiving my mother for moving me was no longer something I struggled with. She wanted to be with her new guy. I wanted to be here. It had been a good fit. My life before Lawton had been dull. Boring. Safe.

Here, in just one week, I'd found a world full of wonder and excitement. How was that bad? Why wouldn't my dad be happy about all this? He had been just as worried about my adjusting to Lawton High School. This should have made his life easier. Yet he was acting like I'd committed some crime.

I was seventeen. Riding in a car with a boy was allowed. We hadn't even been alone. I was getting into full rant mode in my head when we pulled into the driveway and parked. I knew he was going to tell me exactly what I had done that broke the rules in this house once we got inside. Part of me wanted to walk as slowly to the door as possible just to prolong it. The other part wanted to get this over with so I could text Ryker. Apologize to him for my dad.

Needing to talk to Ryker won out, and I stalked to the door with fast, purposeful strides. With a jerk, I opened it and went inside the house, then spun around to wait on my father. He took his time, and when he finally entered, he looked at me standing there. His face was no longer angry. Just set, as if his decision was made. There would be no arguing.

He closed the door behind him while looking at me. Then he said, "You will not date a black boy."

I stood there stunned. I knew Hunter had said this would be an issue, but him confirming it was like being slapped in the face with stupidity.

"What?" I said aloud. I just gaped at him. How could an educated man say something so ridiculous?

He signed this time as well as said it, to make sure I understood correctly, I suppose. "You will not date a black boy."

I blinked. I was at a loss for words. I blinked again. This was not how my mother had raised me. Skin color was not important. Why did he seem to think it was? Where had his ideas gotten so screwed up?

"How is his skin color a problem?" I asked, trying to make sense of this.

"They're different than we are. There are social impli-
cations, Aurora. Just because your momma raised you not
to see color doesn't mean it's not there. You date a black
boy, and you're seen differently."

I gaped at him. Did he believe what he was saying? How
could he think that way? Surely he knew how ludicrous
that sounded. "You can't be serious," I signed and said.

"I don't answer to you, Aurora. You live in my house.
You are my daughter. You will not date a black guy. That is
the end of this discussion."

The fury that crawled all over me with his words came
out in a blast of hot anger as I said, "I'll date whoever I want!
If there are backwoods people like you here that judge me for
it, then they aren't worth their opinion. Skin color doesn't
make you different. And after meeting his family, his father is
a much better man than you are. I would rather be known as
Ryker's girlfriend than your daughter."

His eyes widened for a moment, but then he just walked
past me as if I hadn't said a word. I stood there watching
him go, and after he turned the corner to go upstairs to
his bedroom, I sank down on the nearest chair. He hadn't
been open to anything. That was his way of saying I had no
power here.

This wasn't over.

CHAPTER 35

RYKER

He had taken her, and I couldn't do a damn thing about it. I don't know how long I stood there staring at the darkness his SUV had driven off into when Nash put his hand on my shoulder. "Come on. You need a drink," he said with a firm squeeze.

I shook my head. "No. I don't. Give me a ride to my house," I told him finally, turning to get back inside Tallulah's car. Our vehicles were at the high school, but I wasn't in the mood to go get mine tonight. I wanted to go home and wait for her text.

Nash didn't argue with me. I heard him saying something to Tallulah, but I didn't listen. I didn't care. Nothing

here mattered. Not now. I thought of Hunter and looked
out toward the field that had already started to fill up.
Music was blasting, and voices were growing louder.

"Is Maclay here?" I asked no one in particular.

"No idea. But you need to keep your distance from
the Maclays," Nash said, his tone laced with dislike. He'd
known as well as I had that Aurora's dad hadn't been happy
about her being with me and why.

"That's not going to happen. You know I can't stay
away from her."

Nash sighed but said nothing. We both climbed into
Tallulah's car and remained silent most of the way to my
house, which was only a mile away. I knew he wanted to
give me advice, but I also knew he wasn't stupid enough to.
Because of this, there was nothing to say.

When he parked in front of my house, I thought I was
going to get out with a *thanks*, but he said something first.

"Is she worth it?"

I paused and then turned my head slowly in his direction. "Abso-fuckin'-lutely."

A grim smile touched his lips, and he gave me one small
nod.

I climbed out and closed the door without saying any
more. My parents would be getting ready for bed and not
expecting me home so soon. They'd have come straight

home after the game and known I'd be at the field until late. Answering their questions about why I was here wasn't something I wanted to do. I would face that later. Tomorrow. Not now.

Instead I went to the cellar door that led into the basement. The den would be empty. Nahla never came down here at night. The lack of windows scared her. I had used it to sneak in and out of the house since I'd figured out how to get past the lock on it when I was twelve.

Tonight it wasn't locked. I didn't remember unlocking it lately. I hadn't been using it. I lifted one side of the metal door and climbed down the short ladder to the ground. It was like a small underground closet of sorts. The floor was cement, as were the walls. Only enough room to turn around. It wasn't even large enough to spread my arms out straight on both sides.

I reached for the wooden door that led into the basement den, turned the knob, and walked into the room, expecting darkness. But the gas fireplace was on, and my father was sitting in the recliner that faced the door I had opened. He wasn't watching TV or reading. He was sitting there with his arms crossed over his chest and his right ankle propped on his left knee as if waiting for someone.

It didn't take me more than a split second to realize the someone he was waiting on was me. That explained the unlocked door. I stood there a moment and wondered if there was any possible way he knew about tonight. It had only just happened. Did he even know Aurora had been in the car with me on the way home? We hadn't discussed it.

"Hey," I finally said, breaking the silence.

"Have a seat, Son," he replied.

I closed the door, and then looked back at him. "How'd you know I'd be coming in this way?"

He looked amused. "You've been sneaking in and out of that door for years. After tonight's run-in with Maclay, I figured you'd come on home and not want us to know."

Damn. Word traveled at lightning speed around here. I knew it spread fast, but I figured it would at least be tomorrow morning before they knew. I walked over to the sofa and sank down onto it, realizing I wasn't upset he was here waiting on me. Seeing him was a relief. I needed advice. I needed my dad. He had known that. He always seemed to know.

"It sucked," I said honestly, feeling the tightness in my chest at the image of Aurora walking away from me and my trying to stop her dad. Telling him we'd done nothing wrong. That I respected her and would never do anything to harm her. He'd told me to stay away from his daughter and left.

"I heard he was a jackass," my dad replied.

"How did you hear about this so soon? It literally just happened."

Dad tilted his head to the side. "Did you honestly think I let you throw parties at a field with a bunch of teens and not have eyes and ears there? Just like this escape door you use to sneak in and out of? It's my house. To keep the people inside of it safe, I know who comes and goes in this house. Just like I know what goes on out there at that field. I protect what is mine."

Eyes and ears at the field? Who the hell was that? For a moment my mind was taken off the situation with Aurora, but that was a brief moment only. I would figure out my dad's secrets another time. It really wasn't important right now.

"You had parties out there as a teen," I pointed out. Wondering if my grandpop had also had surveillance and shared it with his sons once they had sons of their own.

Dad smirked. "And you think your grandpop didn't have his hand on that? Shit, boy, we'd have been arrested a dozen times if we hadn't known Daddy knew it all. We kept it clean."

Shaking my head, I would have smiled if I wasn't so damn tore up about Aurora.

"You just met the girl Monday. I've pointed that out already. I agree she's a beauty and seems sweet. Didn't get to really know her. But you are now faced with the reality you knew was there waiting on you. She's a white girl with a father who doesn't want her with a black man. It's typical around here. Don't seem to matter that I make more money than he does or that my ancestors were some of the first to settle in this town. Not as slaves, either. As free men and women. You got to decide if she's worth this fight."

I didn't wait for him to say more. "She is. I've never felt this way about anyone. I didn't think it was possible. But I'd give up anything to be with her. To see her smile. She's everything I want to be. She makes me want to be a better person . . . just being near her makes me wish I'd never been the guy I was before."

He looked somewhat disappointed by that. "You're headed to State. You know good and well the way the two of you play together on the field will be the main factor in winning State. You're gambling a state championship for a girl you will have to leave this summer."

Talking about leaving Aurora was the last fucking thing I wanted to do right now. "Hunter doesn't agree with his father."

Dad frowned as he was thinking that through. "He's a smart kid. I already knew that. But his dad controls him. The boy is so under that man's thumb it's sad. Not sure he's going to stand against his dad on this."

I ran my hand over my head and sighed in frustration. "Why does this have to be so hard? I respect her. Hell, I love her. I think I did the moment I saw her. It was a crazy-ass pull the first time I looked at her—I can't explain. But I don't want to lose her over her dad being a fucking racist."

The firm line of my dad's mouth tightened. "I had this same damn talk with your uncle years ago. I was so mad at him for giving up everything for a girl, I didn't speak to him for months. We had our futures planned. We'd worked toward them, and all he had to do was give her up. But he didn't. He said his heart was where she was, not on the field. Her daddy thought he could end them by taking her away. Moving her. But your uncle gave it all up and followed her. Just about broke your grandpop's heart in the process. He had farmed this land and worked hard to give us a life he didn't have. That was the son who would go all the way. The one with the talent to play in the NFL. And one white girl with a racist father determined to keep them apart changed it all." Dad paused. I knew this story well. Nash and I had heard the way his father had given up everything to chase his mother across the country and win her back. But right now I realized it made sense, and I needed any wisdom I could get, so I shut up and let Dad talk.

"Your uncle made the right decision. She is his one and only love, and they've had a good life. They're still happy.

The NFL would have been a sweet life too, I imagine, but if he'd chosen it over her, I think he'd have ended up empty and sad in the end. Money and fame can't buy happiness. Not the long-term kind. I'm telling you all this, although I know it's a story you're familiar with, because I'm afraid it's what you're weighing your decisions on. Their past and what they have today." Dad dropped the foot he had propped up onto the floor and leaned toward me. His expression serious. "Your uncle loved your aunt from the time they were kids. He didn't meet her and make a decision on his future after only one week. He knew what it was like to have her and what it was like not to have her. His decision was one with history behind it. You have no history with Aurora, Son. You can't be in love after only a handful of days. Love doesn't work like that. It takes time. It takes really knowing someone. It isn't a pretty white smile, and freckles on pale skin, and fiery red hair. It's deeper than all that."

My first reaction was to jump up and argue that I loved Aurora and he didn't understand, but I didn't do it. I sat there and let his words sink in. I didn't agree with him about love, though. I wasn't in love with Aurora's appearance, although she was nice to look at. I knew telling him that wasn't going to get through to him. He was a firm believer I wasn't in love with her this soon.

"Choosing to be with Aurora isn't giving up my future.

I'm not going to let it affect my performance on the field next week. Truth is, losing her would affect it more than anything. I still plan on going off to college, playing football, and doing all those things I planned. But I can do that and still be with Aurora. I can achieve all of that with her in my life."

Dad stared at me a moment. I knew he disagreed. He didn't have to say it; I could see it in his expression. "What if she doesn't want to fight to be with you? What if standing up to her father isn't worth it to her? How will you handle that?"

This was something I hadn't thought of, because I didn't even think it was a possibility. I opened my mouth to say so when my phone dinged in my pocket. I quickly pulled it out, wanting it to be her. Now more than anything needing to hear from her. Know she was okay.

I'm so sorry about tonight. My dad was awful and I can't apologize enough for him. I left only because I wanted him to stop making a scene. It was your night to celebrate with the team and he was ruining it.

I read the words three times before lifting my head to meet my father's gaze. I was smiling and hadn't realized it. She wasn't running from me or shutting me out. Even letting the doubt creep in made me feel guilty. I knew her better than my dad understood.

"That her?" he finally asked when I said nothing.

I nodded.

He waited. I made him wait. Just to make a point, I guess, or because a part of me was pissed with him for making me doubt her feelings for me. That was a head game I wasn't sure he even knew he was playing. Or maybe he did.

"She's sorry about her dad. She's embarrassed and said she left so he'd stop making a scene and ruining my night to celebrate with the team." As I told him what she'd texted, I didn't look away from him; I held his steady, firm gaze.

He sat up, then slowly stood. I thought it was over, and he was done. I was wrong. "She's a sweet girl, like I said. But she's only now getting a taste of the fight ahead of her. You can't be sure she'll survive it or want to even try. You. Just. Met. Her." He said the last four words slowly and with a hardness in his voice, as if he couldn't get me to comprehend that one fact.

"I. Love. Her," I responded.

What Are You Doing
Right Now?

CHAPTER 36

AURORA

I understood why you left with him but I have no desire to celebrate without you. I left right after you. I'm at my house. Are you okay?

His text made me sink onto the bed with relief. Why him leaving the field made me feel better I didn't want to think about too much, because it made me selfish to feel that way. He should have gotten to celebrate. I shouldn't have ruined it. But the fact he left after me also made me smile. Maybe because it was late, or because my dad had acted so awful, my emotions were all over the place, and I felt tears sting my eyes.

I'm okay. He didn't say much more. I just hate he messed up our night. Especially yours.

I sent it and then wiped at the tears rolling down my face. I wasn't even sure why I was crying. There was so much going on right now I didn't know what had upset me the most. I had almost texted my mother, but I hadn't. I would tomorrow. See if she had advice or if she even cared.

He ended my night earlier than I wanted but he didn't ruin it. The ride home with you was perfect. It was all the celebrating I needed. Just getting to hold you was amazing.

My tear-streaked face flushed pink as I read his words, and my sadness was instantly transformed to joy. That easily. Was this the way love was? Did it mean you could be snapped from one emotion to another with simple words? It felt like I was on a roller coaster, and not knowing what was coming next was exhilarating, even when it was scary.

I thought I might have messed up the ride home. I didn't mean to embarrass you in front of Nash and Tallulah. I should have been more thoughtful of their being in the car.

I erased and rewrote that text three times before sending it. I had to address this now, or I'd stay up thinking about it and worrying that I'd done something wrong.

You didn't embarrass me, Aurora. You had me so damn worked up I wasn't sure if I should tell them to park the car and get out or thank my lucky stars for whatever I'd done to have you in my lap. I stopped you because I was afraid if we kept going I'd go too far. I wanted to. So very bad.

My heart raced as I read his words, and I squeezed my thighs together from an unexpected tingle there. Much like the one in the car when I'd managed to twist and straddle his leg. I had been so desperate to get closer to him, I hadn't meant to do that exactly, but it had happened in the cramped confines of the backseat. Then the way it had felt had been so wonderful I forgot everything around us and was lost in the moment.

He was right that I'd have been embarrassed later. I just hadn't cared at that time. He was protecting me even when he wanted more. My smile was so wide now my cheeks hurt.

I thought I had gone too far. It just happened. I wasn't thinking. I didn't really want to think, to be honest. Things felt too good and I wanted to feel more.

That was by far the most racy thing I'd ever said or texted. I battled sending it, but I figured I'd straddled his thigh tonight and put his hand up my shirt; this wasn't worse than those things had been. I sent it. Then waited anxiously. Not sure how he would respond, but knowing it would make me miss him and wish I hadn't been forced to leave tonight.

It was probably a good thing I never got you to the barn tonight. You deserve more than a barn and I want you to feel respected and cherished. The way you're talking I'm not sure I'd have been able to keep being noble once I had you alone.

I was squeezing my legs together again. My breaths were quick and a bit erratic. My imagination went to being alone with him in a barn. No one to see us. I wondered what all the other things would feel like. Did it get even better than the little I had experienced in the car?

Sex was never something I'd thought about. I'd never imagined it with anyone. Until now. Was this normal? Did Tallulah and Nash have sex? My mother never talked to me about it, and all I knew was it had gotten a girl pregnant back at my old school, and she'd left to go raise her baby without help from the guy who had gotten her pregnant. I always thought there must have been some trauma in her life to make her want to have sex with a guy so carelessly.

I had judged too soon. Maybe she'd loved him.

We may need supervision until the State game is over. Right now all I can think about is, never mind. I won't say that. Just knowing you want me too is making this harder than I ever imagined.

His text once again had me giddy and silly. As if this night hadn't been awful just an hour earlier. I kicked off my shoes and slid out of my jeans, took off my sweater and bra, grabbed a T-shirt from beside my bed to put on, then slid under the covers before texting him back.

What are you doing right now? Other than texting me?

I sent it knowing that was safe and would get us on a less naughty topic.

It took only seconds before he responded.

Lying back on the sofa in the den watching the flames in the fireplace and thinking about how just talking to you fixes everything. This is better than the field.

I could picture him there, lying on the sofa I had sat with him on just last night.

I wish we had made it to the field. I wanted to celebrate your win with you there.

Getting to experience something that was that big of a deal to him was important to me. Hunter wasn't here, so he must be there. Which was unfair. Ryker won that game just as much as Hunter had.

We wouldn't have made it to the field, Aurora. I think I'd have kept you in the barn kissing those sweet lips all night.

That answer made me wish that had happened. I sighed and thought of how good it felt to kiss him.

It was after two when my eyes finally closed with my phone still in my hand. I dreamed of Ryker, the backseat of a car, and other things.

CHAPTER 37

RYKER

The last text I got from her was at two fifteen a.m. Her silence had meant she'd fallen asleep. I'd finally put my phone down after ten minutes and done the same. I was exhausted. When I'd woken up around eleven the next morning, I expected to have a text from her. But there was nothing. I waited until after twelve to send her a "Good morning, beautiful" text, although it was afternoon at this point.

No response. I stopped staring at my phone and went to the kitchen to fix a grilled cheese sandwich and sat down with a bag of Doritos while waiting for her response. When my phone finally lit up, it was Nash, and I was annoyed when I picked it up to read his text. Not because I had an issue with him, but because he wasn't Aurora.

Taking Tallulah to see the Christmas lighting tonight in town. You and Aurora want to come with us?

Thanksgiving was next Thursday. The town of Lawton always lit up the streets downtown with Christmas lights the Saturday night before Thanksgiving. I'd forgotten about it, because I hadn't been to the lighting event since I was a kid. However, Aurora would enjoy it, and I'd enjoy doing anything with her.

That is if things are okay and she can get out of her house.

That was the next text when I hadn't responded yet. The fact she still hadn't texted me concerned me. I wasn't sure what was going on, or if she was just still asleep.

I'll let you know, I sent back before he could start hitting me with questions I didn't know the answers to just yet. I found it hard to believe she was still sleeping.

Don't do anything stupid. Just 2 weeks until State. Don't fuck up.

I wasn't responding to that text, but he knew I wouldn't. He was being an ass. I finished off my lunch and cleaned up my mess, or my mother would have me in here cleaning the kitchen with a fucking toothbrush when she got home. I had made that mistake a few times. She made sure each time the punishment was worse. She was a small woman, but I feared her.

When it was almost one and there had been no response, I made up my mind to get dressed and go to the damn Maclay house myself. I wasn't scared of her dad, and I'd like a chance to get through to him that I wasn't bad for his daughter. I wasn't the guy he assumed I was. My skin color didn't define me. I would spend forever making myself worthy of Aurora, and if I could just tell him that, then surely he'd believe me. He'd listen. I loved his daughter. I would do anything for her. The difference in our skin didn't mean a damn thing. I could make him see this. He just needed to know how much she had changed me.

Nahla was coming down the stairs with her face in her phone when I headed for the door.

"Where you going?" she asked. Neither of our parents was home, and she hated staying here alone. Not because she was scared, but she was bored. I wasn't taking her with me to do this, though.

"To talk to Aurora's dad," I said without pausing.

"Uh-oh, I heard about that."

I didn't even ask how she had heard about it. I figured the whole town knew about it by this point. There had been enough witnesses to talk last night.

"Lock the door behind me," I called out, and closed it firmly.

Now that I had decided to do this, I was ready. I didn't

like hiding from shit. I faced it and conquered it. I sent Aurora a text in case she was awake and had not been able to respond yet. I couldn't think of why she wouldn't, but I knew she had a reason.

I'm on my way to your house. I'm going to talk to your dad.

After sending it, I pulled my truck out of the drive and headed to her house. My dad wouldn't agree with this. I already knew that. But I didn't care, and if he knew I was doing it, he wouldn't stop me. He'd taught me to be a man and handle my problems. That was what I was doing. Aurora's dad just needed to get to know me. See I was serious. I respected his daughter. Since I hadn't told her I loved her yet, I wouldn't tell her dad that.

I didn't think he'd react to that as well as my dad had. He may send her to live with nuns. Smirking at the ridiculous idea, I turned the radio up and cleaned my head of anything else. I could do this. There was no reason to be nervous. I spent the short trip with an ongoing pep talk and glancing at my phone for a response from Aurora.

When I pulled into her drive, there was still nothing. Hunter's truck was in the drive, but I didn't see her father's SUV. Didn't mean it wasn't in the garage, though. Regardless, I knew someone was home. And if Aurora wasn't responding, I needed to know why. There was always the chance someone had told her some of the bad shit I'd done in the past.

That made me sick to my stomach. She'd eventually hear things, but I was hoping when she did, she'd let me explain. Tell my side of the story. Which wasn't that great. Basically, I was a jerk. I'd messed up a lot. If I'd only known I'd meet her one day, I would have been much different.

I wasn't even to the front door when it opened, and I saw Hunter standing there. He looked serious. He definitely didn't look like he had good news to tell me. It was the exact opposite. That made me pause in my step. What was I about to walk into? Was she mad at me? Was her brother here to stop me from getting to her? Fuck, I hated this. Not knowing.

"She's gone." He said the words before I reached the door.

I stopped completely then. "Where?" I asked, thinking maybe she'd gone with her dad somewhere today to talk. Was he not letting her text? He possibly took her phone away while they had one-on-one time.

"To our grandmother in North Carolina."

That took a minute. I stared at him, thinking I'd heard him incorrectly. Why had he sent her back there? Was it where she had lived with her mother? Was he leaving her there?

Denver was there.

"What?" I asked, wanting to be wrong. Wanting the fear now clawing inside my chest ready to erupt and cripple me to go away.

"Dad took her to the airport early this morning. Put her on a plane."

My knees felt weak, and the next intake of air was difficult. It was like I had been punched in the stomach or, worse, I'd been hit with an illegal tackle by a defensive lineman leading with his head straight to my gut. I couldn't talk. Breathing was hard enough. Motherfucking North Carolina was too far.

"He took her phone before she woke up. Read her texts. Then packed her bags. I didn't think he'd be this extreme. Neither did Aurora. We were wrong." He said it as if he was apologizing.

"She's coming back, right?" I was grasping now. He couldn't just leave her there. If that had been an option, she would never have been brought here. Right?

"Yeah, Gran won't be able to keep her. It's just for the Thanksgiving break. Dad said Aurora needed space from . . . you . . . and to see her old friends." He said it with reluctance. He wasn't saying Denver's name, but it was there, hanging in the silence. We both stood for several moments, letting his words sink in. Then he said, "I'm sorry. I can tell you care about her. I told Dad as much, but it didn't matter. He said she's confused."

I took a step back and felt white-hot anger well up inside me. "Because I'm fucking black? That's it? My skin color means that much to the man?" I was yelling. I didn't care. Let the neighbors hear me. Nothing mattered right now. Not one goddamn thing. All that mattered was on a plane headed northeast.

Hunter didn't respond, but I could see the shame on his face. He wasn't like his dad. I couldn't stay here. I couldn't go home. I didn't want to be anywhere. She was gone for a week. That was all, but she was gone back to her old life. Where Denver was. Where she fit in easily. Where friends who were also deaf lived. I was here. Without a way to talk to her.

"Will she have a phone there?" I asked, praying Hunter was going to help me with this. I had to have some hope. I'd just found her, and I couldn't lose her.

"I'll get you the number if she does. Mom isn't in agreement with Dad's decisions. I spoke with her two hours ago on the phone. Gran doesn't know the exact reasons Aurora is being sent to stay with her this week. Mom is going to tell her, and she's not gonna be real happy with Dad about it. Problem is, Gran still has a landline phone. I don't think she'll be getting Aurora a cell phone for the week. Gran also doesn't have internet, so Skype is out."

Fuck!

She was going to be out of my reach for a week. I had no way of knowing if she would change her mind, if her feelings for me were strong enough, if she'd realize Denver was better for her. That was hard to think about.

"She cares about you," Hunter said as if he knew what I was thinking. "She didn't want to go," he added. I could see there was more he wanted to say, but he didn't. I just nodded, because I couldn't say anything. My throat was so damn tight it was painful.

With one last apologetic glance, he closed the door. I looked up at the window Aurora had told me was hers. Knowing she wasn't there was so damn depressing I couldn't stand here anymore. I had to get away. From this whole goddamn town. They all knew about last night. They'd all want to say something to me about it.

I couldn't talk about this. I knew it was only a week. She was coming back to Lawton. What I feared was what would happen when she was back. Would her father keep her home? Would she have to do virtual school? Would he ship her off to a hearing-impaired school? Or would she come back and tell me she had been wrong about breaking up with Denver. Because being with him was easier for her.

Was I worth the fight she'd face?

Sulking Won't Fix
Nothin', Honey

CHAPTER 38

AURORA

One week was all it took to change my life. I'd been dropped off at my father's house, never realizing that in seven days I would be a different person. That I'd want things I didn't think I cared about. I found out I was stronger than I'd believed. Braver than I would have ever guessed. I'd also learned confidence I didn't have before. All of this because of Ryker.

He'd made me want more, gave me the desire to step outside my comfort zone, to trust myself and others; but most importantly he made me embrace my differences, not let them stand in my way. I had used my voice without even thinking about it with the airline attendants and even the elderly lady who sat beside me in first class on the non-stop flight to Raleigh.

When I'd woken up to my father standing at the end of my bed with my suitcase at his side, I'd reached for my phone, already knowing it would be gone. He'd refused to give it back to me, even when I broke down and began crying. Being forced to leave without getting to tell Ryker bye had been unfair, but then the entire situation was cruel. Why would I expect my father to act fairly? I had refused to look at him after that. When he'd tried to tell me bye at the airport, I'd walked away from him through security and left him behind without a word or a wave.

I had nothing to say to him. Not anymore. He'd not listened to me plead with him about giving Ryker a chance. When I'd called him racist, he'd taken a step toward me, and although I didn't think he would have hit me, Hunter moved in front of him and blocked his path to me. I would never know what he had planned to do.

Hunter's back was to me, and I had no idea what he said, but my dad had taken a step back. Hunter had stayed by my side then until I was in the car and headed to the nearest airport big enough for nonstop flights to North Carolina, which was a two-and-a-half-hour drive from Lawton.

My gran had met me at the airport and hugged me

tightly. I didn't know how much she knew about the situation, but she was here. The familiar scent of her perfume and the safety that came with being in her embrace brought on the tears I'd been fighting back. She patted my back as I cried in her arms, and I didn't care if I was loud or not.

We stood there like that until I could get control of my emotions; then I pulled back to wipe at my tear-streaked face. She held out a handkerchief she'd retrieved from her purse, which she called a pocketbook. I did the best I could to clear my face from my outburst, then handed it back to her.

"Your father has always been an ass. I just didn't know he was a bigot, too." Gran was my mom's mother, but that wasn't why she spoke about my dad that way. She was just blunt. She'd quickly tell anyone who would listen my mother's faults just as easily.

I gave her a shrug. "Me either," I said. Because, honestly, I hadn't thought he'd react this way.

"Bringing you back here only one week after you had to pack up and move. Shame on him. You need to adjust. He isn't giving you time to do that." Gran was signing now instead of just talking. She always fussed when family expected me to read their lips. She said it had to be exhausting for me.

"He thinks me being back here will be enough to end my feelings for Ryker," I told her.

She raised one white eyebrow. "Will it?"

I shook my head. "No."

She gave a firm nod then. "Good. Because Denver is coming over for dinner tonight. Your dad wanted you to be immersed in the friends you left behind in hopes of ending these feelings you have for Ryker. We will immerse you, then show him it won't work." She signed this with an expression on her face that said she truly believed it.

But I was shaking my head when I said, "NO!" using my voice. I didn't want to see Denver. The time I'd spent with Ryker might have seemed like a long time, but it hadn't been. I'd only been broken up with Denver for a few days. Seeing him now was weird.

"He was happy to come. I can't take back the invite now," Gran said with a frown.

I moaned and covered my face with my right hand. This was going to be a train wreck. "We broke up," I told her, dropping my hand from my face.

She shrugged. "I know that."

We made it to baggage claim, and I found my luggage on the carousel without looking at Gran. She was serious about manners, and I knew she wasn't going to cancel tonight. Dinner with Denver was the last thing I needed to deal with right now. I was still facing a week stuck here with no way to talk to Ryker and explain.

I wasn't sure Hunter would do it properly, and without a phone or internet, I didn't know how I was going to communicate with anyone in Lawton. My dad didn't seem to care about that, though. This would have been the first Thanksgiving I'd spent with him in four years, and he'd sent me off. I hoped he enjoyed the tofu turkey Ella would feed him.

Rolling my luggage out of the airport, I followed my gran outside to the much cooler weather than what I had left this morning in Alabama. The sunlight made me squint, and I found my sunglasses in my purse, then quickly put them on before hurrying to catch up with Gran, who walked way too fast to be seventy-two years old.

The familiar blue 1988 Lincoln Town Car was parked in a handicapped parking spot, and I rolled my eyes. Gran thought that her age made her handicapped, when she walked faster than I did, and several miles a day at that. She opened the big trunk, and I put my suitcase in there before closing it and going to get in the passenger seat.

The car smelled like vinegar and apples. It always had. Gran cleaned everything with vinegar water, but the apple-scented fragrance she sprayed in the car every week clung to the fabric on the seats. It wasn't pleasant, but she didn't seem to agree.

I looked over at her when she still hadn't cranked the car, to see she was watching me.

"Sulking won't fix nothin', honey. Not a damn thing. Suck it up and deal."

I wasn't sulking. I was angry at the unfairness of it all. "This isn't fair," I replied.

She pursed her lips and tilted her head back and forth like she agreed. "Nope, it ain't. But neither is the rest of this life. Might as well figure it out early and get tough."

Get tough. I thought I *was* tough. I didn't say so, though. There was no point in arguing. I leaned back and buckled up as she finally started the car and backed out of the parking spot she didn't belong in.

Life may be unfair, but couldn't we at least trust our own parents to be fair? It seemed a cruel reality that came along with sucking it up and getting tough.

CHAPTER 39

RYKER

The rest of the weekend I stayed home. I didn't want to go anywhere or see anyone. Nash finally left me alone. My dad wasn't saying much about it, and my mother was baking brownies and cookies to try and cheer me up, which meant she was seriously worried. I didn't trust her culinary skills enough to eat any of it, but I also didn't have much of an appetite anyway.

Hunter hadn't called or texted with any info on Aurora.

Nova, Pam, and Mandy had all texted me, though. Each one offering to comfort me in many different ways and making comments about Aurora not being worth my time. I deleted each text, annoyed by the way they insinuated that Aurora was to blame for her father's racist issues. They were another reason I hadn't left my house. I'd face them and more if I went anywhere.

It was Tuesday afternoon before Nash came to my house demanding I get out. He wasn't going to let me stay here any longer. Tallulah was busy baking with her mother in preparation for Thanksgiving on Thursday. Apparently they'd be joining our family dinner at my grandparents' house. I'd heard Mom saying something about it yesterday on the phone with my aunt when they were deciding who needed to bring what to the meal. Tallulah's mother was bringing all the desserts, except for my grandmother's pecan pie, and was bringing homemade bread too.

None of this I cared about.

"I'm not leaving until you come with me," Nash said, dropping down on the sofa in my den and propping his feet up on the ottoman in front of him before crossing them at the ankles. He would leave as soon as Tallulah called. His attempt to act as if he was getting comfortable and not moving was weak. I knew better.

"You want to drive to North Carolina with me?" I asked him. I wasn't joking. I'd been thinking about it since yesterday. My parents would be against it, but I was ready to leave without telling them. I'd call after I was gone and deal with the punishment later.

"Please tell me you're kidding," Nash said.

"Nope."

"Jesus, she's coming back. She's not gone forever. She'll be back Saturday. Right? That's a week. Hunter said she was gone for the week."

That was four days from now, which felt like a fucking eternity. Had she seen Denver? Maybe she would decide to stay with her grandmother. I'd only had five days with her. Denver had years. Could what we had withstand that?

Fuck.

"Some guys are coming over to my place to watch football and get away from visiting relatives in their houses. You're coming with me," Nash said this time after glancing down at his phone to read a text message. This was typical for Thanksgiving holidays. We watched a lot of football and hid from family gatherings until it was time to eat.

Sitting here wasn't helping matters. If I did take off to North Carolina, I wouldn't know how the hell to find her. I didn't know her grandmother's name, and I was positive Hunter wasn't going to give me any help with that. She would be home in a few days. I had to keep reminding myself of that.

Stretching, I looked at my cousin, then gave a single nod. "Fine. Let's go," I replied.

He looked relieved and a little surprised I was agreeing.

I wondered, if I'd pushed him harder, would he have given in to the driving-to-find-her idea. Possibly, but we'd both be in trouble with our parents, and there was little chance we'd find her. I didn't even have a damn phone number I could contact her on.

"Thank God," he muttered, standing up. "I thought I was going to have to talk you out of that stupid going-to-get-her idea."

If I could just talk to her. Know she was okay. Hell, if I could know she wasn't with Denver and hadn't forgotten all about me, that was what I needed. I also wanted to see her smile light up and make me forget everything else.

We made our way back to the front of the house, and as we passed the kitchen, my mom turned and caught sight of us. "Oh good! You're getting him out of this house. I'm tired of his sulking. Take these." She handed me a tray full of cookies, brownies, and some white balls covered in powdered sugar.

"Did you make these?" I asked, unsure if they were going to be edible or if they should be tossed in the trash when we got to Nash's house.

Mom rolled her eyes. "No, Ryker. I did not make those. I bought them from Mrs. Loyola from church. She makes plates full of sweets very year and sells them to raise money for the local toy drive. You should know this by now. Lord,

I've bought too many trays of sweets from her every year since you were a boy."

Mrs. Loyola was about eighty years old, I'd guess, and sat on the front pew at church every Sunday. I didn't make it that much anymore, but I doubted she'd moved from her spot over the years. She always had soft peppermint in her purse, and she'd still give me a piece like I was five when she saw me.

"Yeah, forgot about that," I said as if I remembered we'd gotten sweets from her in the past. I never paid attention to the food in the kitchen or where it came from during the holidays. I just ate it. This was the only time of year we had a stocked kitchen, since Mom thought the holidays meant trays and tins of sweets should cover the kitchen table.

She patted my shoulder and then squeezed my arm. "Go have fun. Don't think about the other stuff. It'll be over soon. All things happen for a reason."

I moved toward the door before Mom could come up with more cliché encouraging words to toss at me. She meant well, but it was annoying. Not even Mom understood how fucking stressful this was. Not being able to check on Aurora. To know if we were still good. I needed reassurance she was coming back. I didn't want life to go back to the way it had been without her.

Mom called out more good-byes as we headed out the front door. Dad was on his way down the sidewalk, dressed in his running shorts and a long-sleeve Dri-Fit shirt. He was sweating even though it was in the forties today. When he saw me leaving with Nash, he looked relieved.

"How many miles this morning?" Nash asked him. My dad ran three times a week and hit the gym two days a week to lift weights. This week he'd run extra, because of the amount of food he planned on eating. He had been complaining about his metabolism being shit since he turned forty.

"Ten," he said with a cocky smirk.

"Damn, you're a machine." Nash knew my dad liked to have his ego pumped.

Dad chuckled, then turned his attention to me. "You getting out. About time."

I didn't respond. I just kept walking to Nash's Escalade.

I Was Lost in a Fairy Tale
of My Own Making
CHAPTER 40

AURORA

What I had come to realize from the moment I met Ryker was made very clear after dinner with Denver. Then early Christmas shopping with him two days later, and a movie night at my gran's with him after making cookies and talking about my old school. Denver was my best friend. There was no desire to touch him or have him hold me. No temptation to kiss him. In fact, we had talked a good deal about Ryker. He'd asked me questions, and I'd been very honest about how I felt.

Denver wasn't jealous or upset. He wasn't that good at acting, and I'd have been able to tell if it had bothered him. Instead he was curious. He seemed happy for me. He also made being stuck in North Carolina for a week bearable.

I laughed with Denver the way I would with Tallulah. Nothing more than friendship stood between us, and it was comfortable.

I didn't tell Denver about the kissing and other stuff I did or felt with Ryker. That was private, but I did tell him how Ryker was exciting and sweet. He even laughed at me for going on and on about what a good guy he was and how no one gave him credit for it. They all seemed to judge him for his past mistakes.

Denver had said during one of my long rants about this that he doubted Ryker considered them mistakes. Which had gotten me into a heated conversation about how he was wrong. Denver had shut up quickly, and that had been the end of that.

Although I did lie in bed that night and think about it. Wonder if possibly Ryker would miss that life. If he'd returned to it now that I was gone. When I got back, would it all be the same? I wanted to text him. I knew Denver would let me use his phone if I asked. I didn't have Ryker's number memorized, since it had been saved in my phone. I was bad about remembering phone numbers. I could ask Hunter. I knew his number by heart. He'd had it for four years.

Every time I considered it, I stopped myself from asking. Not because I thought it would upset Denver. We'd talked about Ryker enough now for me to know he wouldn't mind at all. I almost expected him to offer it, but he hadn't.

I couldn't bring myself to do it, because I was scared. What if Ryker had been with Nova or some other girl? What if Hunter told me something I didn't want to hear? We had just been talking for a week. There was no exclusive thing to what we had. Was there? Did he just want to see me? Or was I supposed to accept him being with other girls?

My stomach would get sick every time I thought about it. Nova's parents obviously wouldn't have a skin-color issue, since their skin color was the same as his. What if he didn't want to deal with me because of my racist father? This time away gave him plenty of space to decide I wasn't worth the trouble. I'd gotten myself so worked up thinking of all these scenarios that I'd lost sleep over it.

"You're doing it again. Zoning out on me," Denver signed as he stepped in front of me to get my attention. We had been cleaning Gran's front porch for her. Tomorrow was Thanksgiving, and she always had a house full of folks. She needed all the available space she could get. Including her large wraparound porch that had more square footage than the inside of the house. My grandfather had always teased her about it when he was alive. Gran preferred to be outside. When they'd built this place, the porch had only covered the front of the house. But over the years, Gran said, my grandfather would add on a little at a time as they could afford it. He had begun by extending the front out six extra feet to widen it. Then he'd gone from there. She would tell me, "Find you a man who will build you a porch bigger than you need and smile while he's doing it. That's the keeper."

I picked up the broom I had set down while wiping off one of six rocking chairs that were on the porch. Then I glanced back at Denver. His family would be here for Thanksgiving too. So would most of the elderly neighbors who had no family around, and any homeless people Gran might come across while out running errands today. It was the way she was. We expected it. I'd met a lot of interesting people over the years.

"You haven't asked me, but here," Denver signed, then took his phone from his pocket and held it out to me.

There it was. He was offering. I'd known it was going to happen eventually. I looked down at the phone in his hand and wondered if this was a good idea or a terrible mistake. I missed Ryker so much. But the fear I'd made all this up to be more than it was terrified me.

"I don't know his number," I signed. "I didn't memorize it."

Denver couldn't sign and hold his phone, but his expression was clear. He knew I could get Ryker's number easy enough. He continued to hold the phone in front of me, waiting on me to take it.

"What if this is a mistake?" I signed. He didn't move.

He wasn't going to let me make up excuses. Denver was one to handle things head-on. Much like he had the ending of our relationship.

I reached for his phone. Dread, excitement, fear all finding a place to swirl together inside my chest and make it hard to breathe. I held it for a moment, and the screen went black. He reached over, touched his thumb to it to unlock it again, then nudged me.

I went to text messages and found Hunter's number already in the contacts. I should have figured he'd have my brother's number.

It's Aurora. How are things there?

I couldn't ask anything more. Not yet.

It was immediate that the small dots appeared to tell me he was texting back.

You're texting me from Denver's phone. Does that mean you're back with him?

I should have explained this first. My thoughts had been on Ryker moving on, not on why I would text from my ex-boyfriend's phone.

No. We are friends. We always have been. Nothing more. He is helping clean up Gran's for tomorrow's big meal she does. You remember those. He offered to let me use his phone to check on things . . . there.

Still I couldn't say Ryker's name. This time he didn't

immediately start texting. That made the sick knot in my stomach get larger, and my throat got tight. Waiting for him to say something was awful. I wanted to text him to *SAY SOMETHING. JUST TELL ME!* But I didn't. My hand was trembling I realized when Denver's hand reached out to steady mine. I looked up at Denver. He signed, "Breathe. It's going to be okay."

I took a deep breath and dropped my gaze back to the screen just as Hunter's text appeared.

You were only here a week, Aurora. It wasn't long enough to solidify things with Ryker. I told you he was a player. I'm glad you're with Denver.

I read that text three times before forcing myself to reply.

What do you mean? Tell me. Don't be vague, Hunter.

I waited on his text, feeling so sick to my stomach I thought I would throw up. I shouldn't have asked him. I should not have said a word. I should have given Denver back his phone and forgot he said anything.

He was with Nova at Nash's place. I was there. I saw him.

I couldn't say more. I'd asked to know. Now I did. I'd never felt so much pain. Handing the phone back to Denver, I waited until he took it from my hand; then I began running. I wasn't sure where I was running to, but I was running away from the words. I'd been right to fear Ryker had been with someone else. He'd gotten over whatever he felt for me when

I was out of sight. I was so naive. Hunter said I was, and I hadn't listened. I had wanted to believe Ryker. He made me feel so alive. But all I had ever known was Denver, and I now understood there was no sexual attraction between us at all. There never was. We were best friends who got confused and thought what we felt was something more.

My feet continued to run as the world passed by me. My face was wet from the tears that had clogged my throat even before Hunter had told me what I somehow deep inside had already known. This was why I hadn't tried to text. I knew it, and if I had known it, then I'd known deep down that it wasn't real for Ryker. Not like it had been for me.

I was one of many. Hadn't Hunter warned me about this? Tallulah, even, the very first day? I had listened to no one. I'd been so sure it was different with me. Why would I be different for him? I wasn't special. Heck, I was more diffi-cult. He couldn't talk to me the way he could other girls. He had to sneak around to be with me. I was one big annoyance. I was work. No wonder he was with someone else this week.

The image of Nova in his arms hit me, and my knees went weak from the pain of it. I slowed to a stop and bent over at the waist to rest my hands on my knees. I was not a runner, and I was now struggling to catch my breath from my sudden need to sprint while sobbing at the same time. This was too much. All of it.

How did it hurt so badly? It shouldn't feel like some-one had hit me in the chest with a baseball bat. But it did. I gasped at the air, and I was just beginning to straighten up when a hand touched my shoulder. I was too tired to jump or even care that I wasn't alone.

Turning, I already knew it was Denver beside me. I stared up at him, wondering if he'd read the text or talked to Hunter himself. Catching up to me would be easy for Denver. He was on the track team at school. Running was his thing. Not mine.

He wasn't even breathing hard. His blue eyes—which most girls at school thought were dreamy and had told me so many times over the years—were full of sympathy. They didn't move me the way the dark depths of Ryker's had. I wasn't lost in them. I could admit they were a clear blue that matched the sky above us, but that was all.

His arms pulled me to his chest, and he hugged me. His chest wasn't wide, and he didn't smell like Ryker's cologne. He was lean, not muscular, and his arms weren't bursting out of his sleeves from defined biceps that belonged on a man. But he was safe. He'd never hurt me. He was my friend who had listened to me go on and on about another boy all week.

We stood there like that until my sobbing subsided. My breathing finally got back to normal, and the tears on my face dried. Although the front of his shirt was now wet.

When I knew I was calm, I stepped back and signed, "I'm sorry." Then: "Thank you." I didn't have the energy for more.

He replied, "You're going to be okay."

I disagreed with him. If I had believed in a fairy tale with a guy so quickly and easily, I was a walking disaster. I couldn't be trusted to make smart decisions.

"I'm an idiot," I replied.

He frowned. "No. He is the idiot."

My first instinct was to defend Ryker, but I stopped myself before I could. Because I no longer needed to do that. They'd all been right. I had been the foolish one. I was deaf, not blind. Yet I'd been so very blind where Ryker was concerned.

I thought about all the times I'd seen him with Nova at school last week and believed it was nothing. Just her trying to talk to him. Then there were the moments I had caught girls winking at him or licking their lips. I assumed it was just them flirting, and he was ignoring them for me. How silly could I be? Why would a guy who looked like Ryker and was leaving to go off to college in the summer want to date just me?

"I was lost in a fairy tale of my own making. That was a lesson, and it won't happen again," I signed to Denver.

He sighed with a subtle lift of his shoulders. "You deserve a fairy tale, and one day you'll get one."

ONE MONTH LATER . . .

*My Days of Playing the Field
Were Done*

CHAPTER 41

RYKER

The weight of the state championship ring on my finger was still foreign to me. I knew I wouldn't wear it after I graduated. It would just sit on a shelf, reminding me of the greatest and hardest time in high school. I wondered if I'd still see her face when I looked at that ring or if one day her memory would fade.

The crowd around me was rowdy and ready for the new year. The clock would strike in less than an hour, and the fireworks would explode over the center of town, while the large ball Lawton dropped each year at midnight on New Year's cast colors into the night sky. It was hard to believe it was almost 2020. I'd graduate in a few months, then move to Oklahoma in late June to begin training.

When I had accepted the football scholarship from the University of Oklahoma over Georgia, Vanderbilt, and Florida, my dad had been surprised, but he didn't argue with me. It had been his dream for me to play football in the SEC. Not necessarily mine. I just wanted to know I was going to play the game. Right now that was all I had anymore. I had tried to find joy in the things I once had, but it was gone.

Just like Aurora.

Nothing was the same after her. I'd played the best game of my life in the state championship. While everyone was praising me, and my name was in the papers with my record-breaking stats, all I could think was *Will this be enough to win Aurora's dad over? Will he approve of me?* I'd played that fucking game, trying to be good enough for a man I didn't even know. I sure as hell didn't like him. But I loved his daughter. I didn't have any doubt in my mind about that now. Her staying in North Carolina had destroyed me.

I'd seen Hunter watching me at school and at the field. He always looked like he wanted to tell me something but couldn't do it. Or wouldn't. I was too damn scared to ask him. If she was with Denver, then I didn't need to be told. Her not returning had been enough.

"Smile, man. It's about to be 2020! The year our lives begin!" Nash had been drinking. I smelled the beer on his breath. Tallulah was snuggled up to his side, keeping warm, and I knew she was sober. She'd drive him home.

I forced a small, tight smile at my cousin. My thoughts weren't on the celebration going on around me. I was here simply because sitting home alone was too much. I thought about her. Always about her.

"Hunter told Blakely to fuck off earlier. Hunter Maclay actually said 'fuck off,' and to Blakely! God, I wish you'd heard it. Funniest shit ever." Nash was so damn happy. Good for him. He deserved it. But did he have to come spew that shit all over me?

"About time he got a backbone," I said, not surprised he'd gotten smart enough to end things with Blakely. She was poison.

Nash leaned over and kissed the top of Tallulah's head. I had to look away. Too painful to think about. They reminded me of Aurora. I was trying to think of anything else. Bring in the new year with a new attitude. It was my resolution. The only one I'd made. Actually, the first one I'd ever made for a new year.

"Happy New Year, Ryker," Nova said as she stepped in front of me. After my drunken behavior the Tuesday of Thanksgiving week she had kept her distance. She'd shown up at Nash's place and been dressed to get attention. I'd had too many beers and made a comment about her not having on a bra. She'd thought that was an invitation and pressed against me before kissing me hard on the mouth. I'd been taken by surprise and slow due to the beer, but I'd gotten her off me, then taken her downstairs and sent her away. Telling her I was in love with Aurora and to please leave me alone. Move on with her life.

She had. She'd started dating Brett Darby exclusively almost immediately. Everyone seemed to think I would care after what they'd seen at Nash's, but they had all gotten the wrong idea that day. Everyone but Nash that is. He knew I'd sent her home, then gone inside his house to sleep it off in his bedroom. He'd found me there that night.

"Happy New Year to you, too," I said, not even attempting a smile. It wasn't in me.

She looked at Nash and Tallulah and said the same thing. Just when she was turning to go, I heard a voice say my name that caused my heart to stop. Literally the sound made it skip a beat. Afraid I had imagined it, I spun around so damn fast that if I had been drinking, I would have fallen on my ass.

Green eyes, freckles, with red curls bound up by the scarf around her neck. Everything around me went silent. I felt like I was standing in one of my dreams.

"Aurora." I said her name, afraid I'd finally lost it and made her up. If I blinked, she'd be gone. I didn't fucking blink.

"Hello," she said. It wasn't as soft as she used to speak, and it was clearer . . . different.

Her cheeks were flushed pink from the cold, and her perfect nose was equally pink. I stood there frozen, remembering it was my turn to say something.

"You're here," I finally blurted out, my eyes burning from not blinking.

She smiled then and nodded her head slightly as if my comment was funny. I finally blinked, and she didn't vanish. I inhaled sharply; this was real.

"Happy New Year," she said, and again I noticed the difference in her voice. She was more confident with using it too. I wanted to grab her and hold her and reassure myself she was here, but I'd not heard from her or seen her in one month, two weeks, and a day.

"You're here," I said it again, and then a hand slapped my back.

"Get it together, man," Nash said firmly beside me.

He was right; I had to snap out of this. Seeing Aurora tonight was the last thing I'd expected. I'd even stopped letting myself think about seeing her again. That had only hurt. Wanting something that bad and knowing it was pointless.

"You came back." I said it more for my benefit than hers.

"Yes. I did," she replied with her new, clearer voice. Something was different. Then it hit me. It was dark out here. Not completely. I could clearly see her face, but reading lips with limited lighting was hard on her. She wasn't as close as she used to be when she was reading my lips under the night sky.

"I didn't think you were coming back." I was afraid to ask if she was leaving again. Hunter had said she wasn't coming back. The one conversation we'd had about her when she hadn't returned from North Carolina. I'd shut down completely then. It had taken me weeks to pull myself together. State had been my only focus, and deep down I'd known it was because it was my chance to be worthy in her father's eyes. I'd thought winning might bring her back. In my head I wanted to believe it would. The man put so much importance on football, I had hoped by some chance he would let her come back. He'd decide I wasn't lower than her. That maybe, by some small miracle, my skin color wouldn't be an issue. But she hadn't returned. It had been my dumb fantasy.

"I wasn't sure if I was," she admitted. "But I . . . missed . . ." She stopped then. She didn't say she missed me. I wanted her to say it. I also wanted her to tell me she hadn't stayed away because of Denver. The memory of him made me remember why she had left.

"Couldn't have been me you missed," I snapped,

unable to stop myself. "Not when you had Denver."

Her brows scrunched as she frowned in what looked like confusion. I had been talking too fast. I was torn between guilt from speaking to her so harshly, even though she couldn't hear my tone, and relief she hadn't been able to read my lips clearly.

"I wasn't with Denver. I wasn't in North Carolina. I left there the Saturday after Thanksgiving."

Okay . . . what? I stood there trying to make sense of what she was saying. Where the hell had she been? Hunter said she wasn't coming back. He hadn't said she also wasn't staying in North Carolina.

"Where have you been?" I asked, trying to speak slower. This was important. She hadn't been with Denver. All this time I thought she'd stayed with him because he was easier, she loved him, her father was happier this way, she was happier—I'd thought a million things, and now none of those made sense. Her not returning to Lawton, to me, it was as fucking confusing as it had been that Saturday when she didn't come back.

"California," she said simply.

Her mother was in California. She hadn't been able to move with her mother and her mom's new man. That had been why she'd come here. So how had she decided to move there and why? Had what I'd felt for her been only one sided? Had I made all that up in my head?

"With your mom?" I asked, hoping she'd explain all this and make me understand it. Make the past month of hell go away.

"Yes and no. Didn't Hunter tell you?" she asked me. I was still trying to get used to her voice. The difference was something else I was struggling to understand. Fuck, what if this was all a dream? I'd had several dreams she'd come back. This felt more real. I needed this to be real.

"Hunter told me you weren't coming back. That's it." I was realizing he was supposed to tell me more. My anger with him was tamped down, though, because Aurora was standing in front of me.

She sighed and shook her head as if frustrated about that piece of knowledge. "I should have figured as much. He didn't want to talk about you when I asked. I thought it was just because you were dating other girls."

Dating other girls? "What?" I hadn't been able to even fucking flirt with other girls. Aurora had ruined me.

She gave me a sad smile then. "It's okay. I've had time to think about it all. Understand. I was new to things and naive. We had just met, barely had time to get to know each other when I had to go. We weren't a couple. I'm not upset you were with other girls so soon."

Nothing coming out of her mouth was making any

goddamn sense. "What?" was all I could say.

Aurora's smile was so damn sweet and genuine my knees felt weak. I wanted to grab her and tell her exactly how things had been for me since she'd left. But right now I needed her to tell me why the hell she'd been in California and was she going back?

"It doesn't matter," she said, waving it off like it was no big deal. "I went to California to see a specialist my dad had found. I—" She paused, then moved her hair a bit from her left ear. The hair underneath was shaved or had been. It was growing back but very short. "I've had cochlear implants. I was scared to try, but after . . . after everything that happened with you . . . I wanted a different life. I wasn't scared anymore. . . . You made me brave. You taught me to love who I was. That new things could be wonderful. You showed me that change wasn't bad. It could be the best thing I never knew was waiting on me. Losing you was . . . hard. But I survived. It was you that I thought of when I needed reassurance."

I let her words sink in as the reality of what she was telling me started to all click into place. Her voice, her confidence. "You can hear me?" I asked, unsure exactly what this all meant.

She nodded. "Yes. It's not exactly like you hear, but yes, I can hear you."

I stood there, wanting to grab her and hold her and tell her she was perfect the way she was. I hadn't wanted to change her. I loved her. Whoever she was.

"I was scared of a lot. That was just one of the things. But after . . . you. I decided I could handle anything if I survived losing you."

I moved then. Taking a step toward her, I studied her face, forgetting everyone around us. "Losing me? You left me."

She looked sad. "I . . . I felt more than you did. You were so different. Exciting, beautiful, fun, sweet, and I'd never met anyone like you. I fell too quickly. Got too attached. Thought it was more than it was."

I didn't keep my distance then. I reached out and took her right hand in mine. "Aurora, I was—no, I AM in love with you. I didn't need more than five minutes with you to fall in love. When you were gone, I knew it was love because it felt like you'd taken my heart with you. I don't know what you've heard or what it is you've made up in your head about us. The week we had together—it was real for me. So fucking real I'll never be who I was before you walked into my life."

Her mouth opened to say something, but the crowd's cheers rose too loudly as the fireworks went off, lighting up the night sky. She jumped from the loud noise. See-ing her react to the sound did something to me I couldn't explain. I let go of her hand to cover her ears with my hands. First needing to protect her. Then needing to feel her again. Bending, I lowered my mouth until it touched the only mouth I ever wanted to kiss.

I didn't care if her father was here. I didn't give a flying fuck where her brother was. I would do anything I had to if they'd trust me with her. Allow me to love her. Be with her. When the fireworks ended, I pulled back slowly until her eyes fluttered open to meet my gaze. Then moved my hands from her ears to cup her face. I ran my thumbs over her high, freckled cheekbones. We weren't alone, but it felt like it.

There was no need to speak. The silent language we'd so easily found before was still there. She loved me. She hadn't said it exactly, but I could see it.

"Please don't leave me again." The desperation in my voice she could hear. Her eyes said as much.

"I'm staying. Part of the negotiating with my father was I'd do the surgery. Then I would come back here after therapy, and he'd let me make my own choices. He would have to trust me."

I wasn't sure I was getting this right. "You thought I had moved on. What choices did you think you were negotiating, if it wasn't to date me?"

The little grin that spread across her lips was so damn adorable I wanted to kiss her again. The need to hear what it was she had to say was the only thing that kept me from doing just that. "I said I understood it wasn't enough time for you to feel anything serious for me. I didn't say I wasn't going to come back and do my best to change that."

My grin was as big as hers now. The idea of Aurora Maclay trying to seduce me, or whatever she'd been trying to do, was pretty damn sweet. "What exactly did you plan on doing?"

She bit her bottom lip this time, and I decided she'd have won by just doing that. I was easy when it came to her. She had no idea how easy. "I had a few ideas. Starting with some more racy clothing than I normally wear. California has stores we don't have here in Alabama. I took advantage of that."

I shook my head as I laughed. "You could have worn your brother's clothes, and I'd have seen no one but you."

"Oh." Her response came out in a soft whisper. A puff of breath.

"I'm going to kiss you again. But first I need to make sure we are on the same page this time. I fell in love with you almost immediately. Every moment we were together, I loved you more. When you left, I was with no one. I was, in fact, a complete mess without you. I'm going to the University of Oklahoma this year. If you could do summer school and graduate early, then come join me, I might be able to actually enjoy my first year of college."

Her eyes went from happy to surprised to thoughtful while I was speaking. "I love you too. I didn't know what I was feeling until I thought you had moved on, and it felt like my chest had exploded. And as for summer school . . . is that even possible? Or are you joking?"

I bent down and placed my forehead on hers. Smelling her sweet breath and wrapping my arms around her, keeping us in our own little bubble. The rest of the world out. "I'm honestly not sure, but leaving you is going to be too damn hard now I know how it feels to be without you."

She reached up and touched my cheek with her small, cold hand. "Let's just see how it goes. But you're going to be great at Oklahoma with or without me there. We have our entire lives. Let's not worry about the future but enjoy the right now."

I'd think about it and do my own research on it. I knew I wanted Aurora more than I wanted to play football. But she was right—we had the here and now to make memories.

"Ryker!" Hunter's voice broke into our happy little bubble, and right now he wasn't on my good side. I lifted my head from Aurora's but didn't move away from her or let her go.

My eyes met the steady gaze of her brother, who was standing to the left of us a few feet away. He walked closer, and his face was serious, like it always was.

He stopped when he was close enough that he didn't need to yell over the voices around us. "I'm sorry," he said, and I was wondering if he was going to elaborate or if that simple apology was supposed to cover all the shit he'd had a hand in. Because if she thought I was dating other girls, there was only one person who could have told her that. I was glaring at him.

"I thought she was better without you, because I didn't think my dad would ever agree to her dating you. It was only going to cause her more pain and put a wall between her and Dad. I was wrong. I've always done what our father wanted. She hasn't. I realized . . . I'm not as strong as Aurora. As for what's best for her, I've watched you. You were different when she left. It wasn't just my sister who was hurting. You were too. You make her happy, and she obviously does the same for you."

That's it. He needed to see me suffer to be sure. I wanted to be furious with him for not telling me where she was. But I couldn't. Because, like me, he was protecting her. He wanted her safe, and I couldn't be mad at him for that. Loving Aurora was something that made you do things you normally wouldn't do.

"Okay," I told him. "What about your dad? Any idea how I'm gonna overcome his issues?" I was careful how I spoke about him because of Aurora. He was a prejudiced bastard, but he was also her father.

"He is okay with this," Hunter said, pointing at the two of us. "He's noticed your change too. He was wrong, and although I doubt he'll ever admit that, he knows it."

I couldn't help but think the way I'd played in the State game and how my name had made the papers, then the Oklahoma announcement when I'd committed to them, had had something to do with it. But whatever the reason, it didn't matter. I loved his daughter, and eventually he'd forget skin color and see me for the man I am. Not just the athlete.

I doubted this would go smoothly with him. He'd hear comments from other bigoted idiots in this town. I knew it would happen. Although Aurora didn't care, I worried that he'd make it harder on us again. I'd do anything to make it easier for her. But Hunter was right about one thing: she was strong. She didn't let others define her. A smile touched my face when I thought of her spunkiness. The girl looked like an angel, but she didn't back down when faced with adversity.

I gave Hunter a nod but said nothing more.

"You going to bring her home?" he asked me then.

"Yes," I said, without asking her if that was what she

wanted. I wasn't ready to let her go. I doubted I would be anytime soon.

"Bye and happy New Year," Hunter said before turning and walking away.

I noticed Nash and Tallulah were gone, as well as the others who had been around us. The crowd was thinning, and the town center was now littered with the remains of the celebration. I turned my attention back to the girl in my arms.

"Can I keep you?" I asked her, wondering how late was too late for her dad.

She laughed. "Until one, then you need to get me home. But there's always tomorrow."

I pulled her against me and inhaled the coconut scent of her hair. She laid her head against my chest, and we stood there under the moonlight. My days of playing the field were done.

Acknowledgments

My editor, Jennifer Ung. She waited patiently while it took me longer than expected to finish this one. I am thankful to have her on my team. Also I want to mention Mara Anastas, Nicole Russo, Caitlin Sweeny, and the rest of the Simon Pulse team, for all their hard work in getting my books out there.

My agent, Jane Dystel. Always has my back and I can trust she'll support my decisions. Having an agent is like a marriage. I'm thankful I have the best.

When I started writing, I never imagined having a group of readers come together for the sole purpose of supporting me. Abbi's Army, led by Danielle Lagasse, Vicci Kaighan, and Jerilyn Martinez humbles me and gives me a place of refuge. They have built a community of readers that not only enjoy my books but build friendships and share other great books with one another.

My family. Without their support I wouldn't be here. My kids, who understand my deadlines and help around the house. My parents, who have supported me all along. Even when I decided to write steamier stuff. My friends, who don't hate me because I can't because my writing is taking over. They are my ultimate support group, and I love them dearly.

My readers. I never expected to have so many of you. Thank you for reading my books. For loving them and telling others about them. Without you I wouldn't be here. It's that simple.